CW01678395

Joe Poyer was
graduated from the Michigan State University with a B.A. in Communication Arts, and is at present the Manager of Project Operations for a pharmaceutical company in California, where he lives with his wife and two sons.

He is the author of *North Cape, The Balkan Assignment* and *The Chinese Agenda* all of which were extremely successful.

Also by Joe Poyer and available from Sphere Books

NORTH CAPE
THE BALKAN ASSIGNMENT
THE CHINESE AGENDA

Operation Malacca

JOE POYER

SPHERE BOOKS LIMITED
30/32 Gray's Inn Road, London WC1X 8JL

First published in Great Britain by Sphere Books Ltd 1976
Copyright © Joe Poyer 1968
Copyright © Condé Nast Publications Inc 1966
Published by arrangement with the author's agent

All characters in this book are fictitious, and any resemblance to actual persons, living or dead, is purely coincidental.

TRADE
MARK

This book is sold subject to the condition that it shall not, by way of trade or otherwise, be lent, re-sold, hired out or otherwise circulated without the publisher's prior consent in any form of binding or cover other than that in which it is published and without a similar condition including this condition being imposed on the subsequent purchaser.

Set in Intertype Lectura

Printed in Great Britain by
Hazell Watson & Viney Ltd,
Aylesbury, Bucks

To Susan with all my love
and gratitude

With grateful acknowledgment, Dennis,
for much needed help
and a named, but unnamed, friend

CHAPTER ONE

'You are Dr. Mortimer Keilty?'

Keilty looked up from the scattering of papers and books on the table that served him for a desk. His eyes refused to focus for a moment and he rubbed the back of a dirty, sunburned hand across his forehead.

'Dr. Keilty?' the naval officer standing in front of him repeated impatiently.

Keilty reached over and shut off the tape recorder. The empty reel, which had been spinning for almost an hour, stopped its subdued clatter. He sat back down heavily and regarded the officer across from him with bleary-eyed distaste and absolutely no curiosity whatsoever.

'What the devil do you want?' he asked mildly.

The naval officer, startled, shifted uncomfortably. He tossed his credentials case onto the table so that it fell open to his I.D. card – a practiced gesture he was proud of.

'Hell, James Bond couldn't have done that better,' Keilty said, reaching for the case. The other flushed angrily.

'Lieutenant Commander Michael Redgrave, Bureau of Naval Intelligence,' Keilty read slowly, then tossed the case back. 'So?'

'My instructions are to discuss with you something of the utmost importance to the security of the United States,' Redgrave answered seriously. 'The Bureau of Naval Intelligence, under direct orders from the Pentagon, has reviewed your file and decided that you are the man it needs.' He grinned a friendly, comradely grin, 'Almost amounts to a command, you know.'

'That's nice. Now get the hell out of here so I can get back to my work.' Keilty picked up his pencil stub and began correcting a much edited, dog-eared manuscript.

Redgrave shifted from foot to foot and looked around the cluttered room for a chair. Finding none, he perched on the edge of the rickety table. Keilty looked up.

'Perhaps you didn't hear me. I . . .'

'Beat it,' Keilty said, and went back to the manuscript.

'Now look here . . .' Redgrave exploded, 'either you listen to me or . . .'

'Shall I throw you out in tiny pieces, or will one pulpy lump do?' Keilty stood up and started around the table. He was almost six-two, and weighed well over two hundred pounds. Redgrave looked at the massive bare chest and sunburned expanse of shoulders and retreated backwards to the door.

'Lanahan, O'Malley,' he shouted. 'Get in here!'

The door shot open and two shore patrolmen with rather ugly black service automatics in their hands stepped through, the pistols aimed at Keilty's midsection. Forty-five caliber, standard Colt side arm, Keilty decided, and my, didn't they look purposeful. Bet they could clean up a barroom brawl or a crap game faster than any squadron of marines.

Lanahan, a thickset, muscular individual with a crusty red scar running from ear to ear by way of the bridge of his nose, made the mistake of stepping around Redgrave, so that Redgrave was between him and Keilty for a brief moment. A lesser man would have ignored the unintended challenge. But not Keilty. He stepped quickly to the left, his right forearm sweeping Commander Redgrave up under the chin and catapulting him back into O'Malley. Lanahan, he caught round the gun wrist with his left hand and reversed into a hammer lock, then threw him onto the two sitting on the floor. From there, it was a simple matter to confiscate both weapons and deposit the three sailors in the middle of the gravel path leading to the bungalow.

Keilty went back to his manuscript and the window that opened onto the blue and green reaches of the quiet Gulf of Mexico, and watched the three sailors trudge back down the path. Rather sheepishly too, he decided.

It didn't take long for the U.S. Navy to return. Keilty's mildly alcoholic fog was punctured by the sound of his name shouted over a bull horn.

He went out, blinking in the late afternoon sunshine. Some one hundred yards offshore stood a Coast Guard cutter. Redgrave, looking very unhappy, stood next to a rear admiral on the forward deck. Keilty noted that although no one stood particularly near the deck gun, its canvas cover was unlashed and folded neatly on the deck forward of the mount – and that a two-foot magazine stuck out of the left side.

Keilty sauntered down to the beach and sat down on the edge of the grass, out of the sun. He raised his half-empty pint of Gilbey's London Dry and toasted the cutter.

'You are Dr. Keilty?' the admiral shouted at him.

'Sounds familiar enough,' he yelled back. 'Go on.'

'Dr. Keilty, I am Admiral Rawingson, Naval Intelligence, Washington. We have something very important to discuss with you; may we come ashore?'

'Nope, say what you have to say from there, then beat it.'

'Dr. Keilty,' the admiral shouted again, 'this matter is very confidential.' He looked round at the grinning coastguardsmen with the senior service's disdain for amateurs.

Keilty considered for a moment; he shook out a Chesterfield and crumpled the empty pack, making great show of his deliberation. The admiral respected it. Half a cigarette later, he took it out of his mouth and waved.

'Hi, Jack, how are the girls in Miami since I left?'

'Great, how's Charlie?'

The admiral swung around and stared at the Coast Guard lieutenant on the bridge. Before he could say anything, Keilty hollered, 'Bring 'em ashore, Jack. Tie up at the dock, so they won't get their white bucks wet.'

The sound of the cutter's diesel engines increased as it swung round for the dock. Jack Weston brought it alongside smartly, aft of Keilty's twenty-four-foot overnighter. Keilty took the bowline and snubbed it down.

The two naval officers jumped down on the dock, but Keilty ignored them. Clapping Weston on the back, he led the way up to the patio.

'Sit down, gentlemen, sit down.' Keilty folded into a chair and shouted, 'Margaritta.'

A lithe, dusky-skinned brunette appeared, wearing a very brief bikini. She stopped beside Keilty's chair, and ran a long finger over his ear. Redgrave flushed, Rawingson softened.

'Glad to see you at least put the top on for our visitors.'

'Hmmm,' she said. 'Hello, Jackie, how are you?' She had a dusky voice to match her skin.

'Margaritta, this is Lieutenant Commander Michael Redgrave and Rear Admiral Rawingson. I, uh . . . didn't catch your first name, Admiral?'

'Uh, it's Peter.'

'Fine, Peter, Pete Rawingson, Margaritta. We're very informal here, Admiral, first name basis only,' he explained.

'How do you do, gentlemen,' Margaritta murmured again.

Redgrave managed to get out a strangled sound while Rawingson stood and reached across the table to shake hands. Margaritta let her fingers slip slowly across his palm. Rawingson sat down looking much happier.

'Rustle up something to drink, sexy.' When she disappeared inside, Keilty laughed.

'She's a friend – out visiting for a while.'

Redgrave let out a long, unsteady breath.

'Dr. Keilty,' Rawingson interrupted, 'this is all very interesting, but we have something extremely important to discuss with you.'

'Tough.'

Rawingson looked pained. 'Now look, Doctor, I realize that the Navy has treated you pretty shabbily in the past, but we are prepared to let bygones be bygones.'

Keilty exploded with laughter. 'You're prepared, hell, that's great. I'm forgiven.' He leaned across the table and growled, 'What makes you think it works both ways? You birds kept me going for two years on a project with nothing but a lousy letter of commitment, then decided not to sign the contract after all. Instead, you gave me my walking papers, classified *my* work, rescinded *my* classification, and kept *my* reports. Two years of work for absolutely nothing.'

To fill the sudden silence, Redgrave said brightly, 'Well, ah, we did pay your expenses.' Keilty regarded him in such a way as to make Redgrave look around unconsciously for a hole to crawl into.

'According to the letter of intent, it was supposed to be a cost-plus-incentive fee. I not only lost my shirt, but I didn't even make a profit. For crying out loud, I'm a capitalist. I work for profit. You ask me to work for you, you damn well better pay me. That's why I pay you to protect me from our communist friends across the sea.'

'But, look here, Dr. Keilty, you're a scientist. After all, the Navy did pay your expenses for two years. We realize you did not make a profit, but as a scientist, you're not . . .'

'Shut up, idiot,' Rawingson glared. 'You've . . .'

'You fathead. You imbecilic, unctuous offspring of a slimy . . .' Keilty broke off, breathing hard.

'No one, no one comes to me and says, you are a scientist. As a scientist you should not make a profit because it's indecent. That just isn't done.'

He lowered his voice and went on. 'I will repeat again. I am an American citizen. I am also a capitalist. And the last time I looked it up in the Constitution, I was still guaranteed the right to make a living. Don't come into my home and accept my hospitality and then ask for anything but a personal favor, unless you damn well make it worth my while to waste my time. That's my value – my time – past time in learning what I know, present time in sitting here listening to your insults; and future time, if I take your job. Jackass!' he finished.

Keilty subsided and Margaritta reappeared from the bungalow, swinging towards them, balancing the tray easily against the roll of her hips. She served the drinks and started to fold gracefully to the grass alongside Keilty. He caught her on the way down.

'Beat it, beautiful, men-talk. Give Jack's sailors a treat. Go for a swim off the pier.'

'Nothing doing,' Weston shouted after her. 'You stay away from there. I want those characters in shape to sail that boat to Miami.'

'She swims with nothing on,' he explained to the Admiral. 'Claims it's more natural that way.'

Rawingson nodded sagely.

'Dr. Keilty . . .' Redgrave began.

'Shut up, idiot,' Rawingson repeated in a weary tone. 'If you had read the report I sent down to you, we wouldn't have this mess now.'

'But, sir, I . . .'

'Will you shut up,' he shouted savagely, then turned to Keilty and in a milder tone, said, 'Look, Doctor, I know you are upset about what happened before. But I am here to see that it doesn't happen again. If we could talk to you *alone* for a few minutes, I am sure you will see the significance of what I have to say.' He glared meaningfully at Weston. The coastguardsman started to rise.

'Sit down, Jack. He stays,' Keilty said to Rawingson. 'He's family and besides, I want a witness.'

Rawingson frowned. 'What's your clearance, Lieutenant?'

'Top Secret.'

'Well – all right. Remember it.'

Rawingson put his brief case on the table and opened it. From the pier, long, drawn-out wolf whistles and a faint splash sounded.

'Oh God,' Weston groaned. 'She did it.'

Keilty grinned. Rawingson spread out an extremely detailed map. Keilty did not recognize it at once.

'This is a chart of the Strait of Malacca – Sumatra to the

south; Malaysia, north.' Rawingson pointed out Kuala Lumpur and Singapore. 'I don't have to emphasize to you the importance to world trade – particularly Western trade – of this strait. Four major shipping lanes and numerous smaller ones pass through these straits from the South China Sea, the Indian Ocean, and the Bay of Bengal.' He paused to see if this had sunk in. Keilty was staring at the map. Weston was hunched in deep concentration.

'If,' Rawingson continued, 'this strait were closed to us somehow, it would be a severe blow to our prestige and influence in the Far East.'

'Us, means us and Britain, I suppose?'

'Yes, Doctor, it does, but additionally, Australia, Japan, Scandinavia, et cetera.'

'I thought the British and Australians patrolled this area just to keep it safe for democracy?'

'They do, but in this matter they have asked our help, since it also concerns us. Let me finish setting the stage.'

'Be my guest.' Keilty looked mournfully at his drink, then picked up the admiral's untouched glass.

'If, as I said, we should find this strait closed to us, it would be costly beyond computation. We should have to detour our shipping nearly seven thousand miles 'round Australia from the Pacific, three thousand miles from the South China Sea through the Celebes, Coral, down into the Arafura and Timor Seas and into the Indian Ocean. A delay of weeks and months.

'From the western approaches, we would have to reverse the procedure. And we would have to abandon our economic and shipping influences in the Far East. And if that is the case, we would be finished forever in Southeast Asia. In addition, it would be a ruinous blow to Malaysia and Indonesia. Malaysia alone does an import–export business in excess of eight hundred million dollars per year – the vast majority of which goes through Singapore. And as you can see by the map, Singapore is strategically situated at the head of the strait. During the war, the Japanese tied us up good in the China Sea and the CBI by taking Singapore. With it, they were able to control the entire Indo-China peninsula and what was then the Dutch East Indies. They forced our shipping right out of Southeast Asia and forced us to institute the airlift over the Himalayas and build the Burma Road to get supplies in from the Indian staging areas.'

'Get to the point, Admiral. I know all that. This area is a

British and Australian responsibility and they seem to be doing a pretty decent job, as usual.'

'Yes, well unfortunately, the straits are international waters. In the past few years since the end of the war in Indo-China, communist guerrilla activity has increased tremendously. Malaysia never did quite suppress the communist insurgents. Within six months of the time the United States withdrew from Vietnam, the communists were active again in Northern Malaya. The straits and the Bay of Bengal have become the new Ho Chi Minh trail for men and supplies into the south and across to Indonesia where the PCP is . . .'

'I read the papers, Admiral. The Red Chinese are protesting their innocence everytime someone even so much as hints the insurgent movements are starting up again. And the Soviets are all sweetness and light again as usual. But I got the impression that the Malaysian and Indonesian armed forces were keeping well ahead. So?'

'Just this. Three months ago, the Vietnamese built a scientific research station about thirty-five miles off the eastern coast of Sumatra, almost directly opposite and south of Singapore. The station is located in the Riouw Archipelago, and is shielded on the north, west, and south by several islands. It faces directly up the strait. Since it is in international waters, the Indonesians and Malaysians have both been refused entry or inspection. The Vietnamese claim it is purely a scientific research station to investigate currents in the southern end of the straits in preparation for later oil exploration. As you may know, the currents *are* very tricky.'

Keilty nodded.

'British photo reconnaissance shows an honest-to-God research station there and nothing else.'

'Nuts. Since when have that bunch ever done any scientific research? They wouldn't know what the words mean.'

'Precisely. In addition to photo reconnaissance, the British have also sent two submarines in. The first was warned away; the second, chased out and damaged somewhat by destroyers. It was a nuclear sub.'

Jack whistled. Keilty was looking interested now. The sound of splashing, whistling, and catcalls from the pier went unheeded.

'What about underwater demolition teams?'

'They have sent in three divers to date. None of them have

returned. It would appear that it is impossible to find out what they are doing.'

Rawingson paused and regarded Keilty. 'That's why they turned to us and we have come to you.'

'Ho-ho, so that's it,' Keilty exclaimed. 'The light is beginning to dawn.'

'I thought it would,' Rawingson smiled. 'We are well aware of the subsequent work you have been doing with dolphins since leaving our, well . . . shall we say – employ.'

'Let's not,' Keilty muttered. 'I take it you are interested in Charlie?'

'Tricky, ain't they?' Jack grinned.

'Just a moment, Lieutenant . . .' Rawingson sputtered.

'All right, no internecine quarrels. But I agree with Jack, Admiral.'

'If half of what you claim about this dolphin is true, Doctor, he's just what we need,' Redgrave said seriously.

Keilty stood up. 'Admiral, can I clobber him again, or just refuse him drinks?'

'For God's sake, shut up, Redgrave. One more word out of you and you'll wind up counting gooney birds on Johnson Island for the Interior Department.'

'But I only meant . . .'

'Shut up,' the admiral roared. He breathed deeply for several seconds, then turned back to Keilty, a serious, almost pleading look on his face.

'Look, Doctor, we need your help. This is serious.'

'Me, or my dolphin? And besides, you still haven't told me what the problem is. For all I know, it really is a legitimate research station.'

'Yes, you're quite right. Please sit down.' Rawingson reached into the brief case and took out a sheaf of papers. 'This,' he said slowly, 'is a series of reports concerning the movement of certain high-ranking military personnel in the Vietnamese armed forces.

'To a last man, they have all been trained in Hanoi and Moscow.'

Rawingson paused before going on. 'Both of you,' he said, looking from Keilty to Weston, 'both of you are to give me your word that you will not repeat a word of this to anyone. Very few people know of it, and that's the way we want it kept.' He selected a slim manuscript with the green top-secret cover sheet of the U.S. Government and the maroon cover sheet of the British Government.

'As I explained, and as you know, the straits are of extreme strategic and tactical importance to us. Their protection was just one of the reasons we risked a land war in Indo-China. But, we also found, that short of a nuclear war which could never be justified, we could not hold South Vietnam. But the war did achieve one limited objective, we managed to keep the straits open. So, we took our losses and pulled out. As long as non-communist governments sit astride the straits, Vietnam will never be a major power. And they know it and so do their friends the Russians. We suspect but can't prove that Vietnam is encouraging the rebirth of communist insurgency movements in Thailand, Malaysia, Indonesia and the Philippines, but under much tighter control than ever before. Vietnam took their lumps for awhile from Cambodia and Laos when the local communists refused to play their game but it looks like even that problem is being solved. Cambodia knows that the Vietnamese can make a great deal of trouble for her at a very critical time. China is trying to prop her up but . . .

'It all comes down to control of the straits. Control would not only give Vietnam tremendous leverage but would also allow her to outflank friend and foe alike. And, it would be a huge bulwark against the Chinese. It is beginning to sound as if they have in mind a revival of the old Japanese Sphere of Greater Co-prosperity with themselves playing the Sons of Heaven.

'A greatly entrenched Vietnamese government on the southern flank, just waiting for a funny move and the Russians in the north . . . the possibilities of the situation are enough to make your mouth water if you sit in the Kremlin. So, the first step must be to neutralize the British, Australian, Indonesian and Malaysian fleets in such a way as to neutralize an advantage to the U.S. Seventh Fleet and to destabilize the Malaysian and Indonesian governments and give the local insurgents a hard crack at them. With governments that are at least forced to be friendly, if not in actual sympathy with, the Vietnamese to the south, then Cambodia, Laos and Thailand will have to fall into line. China will then be caught in a huge pincer, encircled if you will and if it comes to war, she would not stand a chance, even with all her hundreds of millions. If her industrial base is destroyed by Soviet missiles she becomes the agrarian society of the last century and easy prey to all comers.

'The specter of the Soviet Union without the counterbalancing threat of the Red Chinese is something we don't want to have to face in the near future.'

Rawingson held up a ticketed folder.

'In this report, gentlemen, is incontrovertible proof that the Vietnamese have succeeded in manufacturing at least one five-megaton nuclear bomb.'

'My, my,' Keilty whistled, 'how dey do spread.'

'We have very good reason to believe that bomb is being planted on the floor of the Malacca strait.'

'How good?'

'Extremely good. The President has directed us to co-operate in every way with the British.'

Keilty and Weston exchanged long, sober looks. Margaritta came running lightly up the gravel path, fastening the top of her bikini. She disappeared into the bungalow, ignored by the four men.

'What good is it going to do them down there?' Keilty asked.

'If that bomb is detonated, it will destroy the British fleet and send billions of tons of radioactive water over the Malay Peninsula. The Vietnamese will have Singapore relatively unharmed. The Malaysian armed forces in combination with the Singapore police will be pushed back into the interior with the loss of eighty-five percent of their bases, munitions and other material. Vietnamese and probably Cambodian troops will occupy the peninsula without much opposition while the Indonesians recover their own losses; Congress, and the Australian and British Parliaments will spend weeks arguing about what it all means by which time, no matter what they decide, we will have been presented with a very effective and clever *fait accompli*.'

'Looks like I called the wrong parties tricky,' Weston grinned. 'My apologies, Admiral.'

'Not a very pretty picture, Admiral,' Keilty said thoughtfully. 'Allow me to fill in the rest of it. You want me to persuade Charlie to scout out this installation . . .'

'And find us a way to destroy it,' Rawingson interrupted.

'. . . and find *you* a way to destroy it. Quite a task for one silly dolphin.'

'You mean, you don't think he can do it?' Rawingson asked quickly.

Weston laughed and got up and went into the house for another bottle.

'Hell, there's no question but what he can do it,' Keilty continued, 'if . . .'

'If . . .'

'If I decide he should, and if I can explain it to him.'

'If you decide he should. Good God, man, this is no time for personal considerations. We need you.'

'Well . . . that's settled. At least now you're saying so openly,' Keilty said, watching narrowly as Jack returned and poured rum into the glasses. He reached out and tipped the bottle, making it run out faster. Jack looked pained as he held it up and measured the level.

'I just wanted to make sure you were asking, not demanding.'

'What did you mean by explaining it to him – who's him?'

'Charlie, for crying out loud, who else. Look, Admiral, maybe this will work and maybe it won't. Explaining things to a dolphin is a little bit different than briefing a bunch of wet-eared naval officers.

'For one thing, dolphins think differently than we do. They have no politics – so they have no concept of good and evil. Evil to them, or what can be translated for evil, is the concept of shark or killer whale – their natural enemies – and then, not all sharks, only those which prey on dolphins.

'In addition, Charlie won't do everything I want him to – only what makes sense to him. And I am going to have one heck of a time trying to explain this.'

Rawingson took a long pull at the drink Weston had poured him.

'It's funny. We had expected a lot of difficulties, even to the dolphin not being able to do the job. But we never expected that the dolphin might altogether refuse.'

'There may be one other difficulty. How extensive will this reconnaissance need to be?' Keilty asked.

Rawingson sat forward. 'We want a Combined Strike Force of Malaysian, Indonesian and Australian/New Zealand naval units to destroy the research station. The Vietnamese know this but are gambling they can finish before we can move. Naturally, none of the governments involved will act until they have proof . . . or figure the odds are running out. The Malaysians have had a lot of pressure put on them by the Vietnamese lately in the South China Sea and they don't want to worsen the situation if the bomb does not exist.'

'You want a comprehensive survey then. What are you looking for?'

'That we don't know. How would you go about planting a bomb in a couple of hundred feet of water – a very precise bomb, intended to do a precise job. We have specially designed underwater cameras and radiation counters to use for this job. We'll strap them on the fish . . .'

'Not fish, Admiral – dolphins are mammals. And he may not take kindly to being loaded up with equipment.'

'Well, in this matter, I'll defer to you – you know best.'

'Well, well, will wonders never cease?' Keilty muttered to himself.

'The problem remains – we must have that information. And there seems to be no other way to get it.'

Keilty stood up. 'Let's go ask Charlie what he thinks. The most he can do is say no.'

The admiral winced, but followed, stumbling over Redgrave, who in his haste to make amends, botched the job of holding the admiral's chair. Rawingson mentally aimed a kick at Redgrave's neatly pressed backside. Keilty led them around the side of the bungalow, past a neat flagstone patio where Margaritta was sunning herself, one slim ankle in the air and *sans* bikini. Rawingson grabbed the Lieutenant Commander by a lapel and dragged him on.

CHAPTER TWO

On the leeward side of the island, Keilty had constructed a series of three shallow pens – much like Olympic-sized swimming pools – divided by cyclone fencing. The pens were each marked off with colored files of nylon mesh curving to a common opening on the seaward side.

He stopped by the middle pen, while Jack walked over to a small shed that housed the generator. When he opened the metal hatch, the sound of a small diesel motor could be heard faintly.

'Jack helps me with these experiments quite a bit,' Keilty explained. 'Charlie and the rest know him almost as well as me. Jack's a better scuba-diver than I am, so he does most of the underwater work.'

'Our reports did not say that he participated in your work,' Rawingson said thoughtfully. 'There seem to be quite a few holes in our *intelligence*,' he finished, turning a baleful eye on Redgrave.

'All set,' Jack called, and came trotting back.

Keilty bent down and reached into the water for a switch set flush with the wall of the pens. A high-pitched squeak sounded, muffled by the water.

'That's the call,' Keilty said. 'It's a tape recording of my voice shouting "Hey, Charlie" over and over again, about four times normal speed. It goes through loudspeakers spaced around the island and out on the reef. If Charlie is anywhere around, he'll hear it and come on in.'

'What happens if he doesn't hear it?'

'It'll keep playing until he does.'

Keilty paused to stare out across the lagoon. A triangular dorsal fin with a thin wake curling up and around was heading towards the pools, about a hundred yards from the opening.

'Better stand back – this is an old trick of his,' Keilty called, stepping back. They could now see a gray torpedo shape shoot unerringly into the mouth of the pool and race up the fifty-meter length between the red and green files of mesh. Ten feet from the edge of the pool, the dolphin slammed around in a flashing broadside that sprayed water over the edge of the pool and the watching men.

'I guess we didn't move back far enough,' Keilty grinned sheepishly. Redgrave surveyed his soaking-wet whites and splotched bucks with dismay.

The dolphin swam leisurely back to the wall and flipped the switch to cut off the underwater call. Then he backed off a few feet and heaved himself half out of the water and onto the sloping edge. Charlie surveyed the four men with his bright eyes, his short, stiff neck twisting from side to side. Keilty sat down next to him with his bare feet dangling in the cool water and thumped the dolphin on the back of his head.

Charlie opened his mouth, revealing four rows of conical, very sharp teeth, and issued a cross between a grunt and a whistle, while Keilty taped a small microphone next to the dolphin's blowhole, clipped an earphone into the dolphin's auditory hole, and fastened another microphone around his own neck. He plugged both microphones into a mixer and tuned it quickly.

'Charlie's microphone feeds through a transphonemator that breaks down his click and whistle speech into the proper pitches for direct translation into English equivalents. Dolphin speech is composed mostly of broad-band clicks between two kc and four kc per second. In the beginning we taught Charlie to speak English more as a test of his intelligence than anything else. The dolphin language, which is quite similar to that of other Cetacea – whales, et cetera – is also quite difficult to produce without the transphonemator. It's a simply structured language, a straightforward "working" language with a small vocabulary of some three hundred different word symbols, each with a single meaning.'

Keilty patted Charlie fondly on the head. 'He's pretty intelligent, he is. He not only learned to use the transphonemator to translate his language symbols – their meaning that is – into human terms, but he invented new dolphin words and added them to his vocabulary at a phenomenal rate.

'We found,' Keilty went on, 'that the whole key to effective and quick communication between man and dolphin lay in the initial use of the transphonemator to come up with enough common symbols to give us a reference ground – a kind of Rosetta Stone affair.

'Once he had learned to speak to *us* so that his language made sense to *us*, we began to teach him to think in word symbols. Charlie describes the thought process as a mixture of English and dolphinese, although neither is particularly suited to the thinking process in this form. His biggest problem, as you might suspect, was in English words that have more than one meaning, such as *hear, here*. So far, he's not come up with any great earth-shaking philosophies, but then he still isn't clear as to what abstract thinking is. He can reason quite well, but not so well where abstracts are concerned.'

'Then you just reverse the translation process in order for the dolphin to understand you?' Rawingson asked.

'No, not at all, or at least not any more. Dolphins speak and hear about four times as fast as we do. This also translates to their movements and perceptions. Dolphins are extremely fast, as are all sea creatures. In the water they are extremely quick because they are essentially weightless and actually have three dimensions to move through, while we have only two – except by artificial means. So they have to be very perceptive and fast.

'Now, because they do hear and speak and because he now knows English, my voice is merely recorded and played back instantly, but four times faster than normal. I am gradually teaching him to understand me without the speed-up process, but it is like trying to understand a seventy-eight record at sixteen rpm. About twenty years ago, Dr. John Lilly down in the Virgin Islands noticed that his dolphins were repeating a series of sounds over and over. When they taped and slowed them down, they found that the dolphins were actually saying words in English, but four times as fast. They also found that these dolphins could understand some words they were saying. But still it is a long way from isolated words to entire sentences and conversations four times as slow as you are used to. In fact, Lilly had a girl live in the same pool with a dolphin for over a year, ten hours a day, five and six days a week. Before the year was up, they understood each other quite well without using any artificial means of communication.

'English is basically a sentence-oriented language – subject, verb, and modifiers for each as needed. On the other hand, a language such as French, where meaning depends on word variation, might be easier to teach a dolphin, as their language is sound-symbol oriented and each sound means a specific thing, and there isn't the logical progression through a sentence as there is in English. Then again, I may be completely wrong. We will have to try it to find out. Chinese, on the other hand, might even be better. It's a tonal language as is dolphinese – with each sound-symbol having essentially one meaning.

'Anyway, Charlie has become so good at using the transphonemator and has developed such a sense of humor that you sometimes forget that it is a dolphin speaking to you. We've installed a TV set and a microfilm reader that he can watch . . .'

'You mean he can read?' Rawingson asked, amazed.

'Of course. Why not? From speaking a language, it's not so hard a step to breaking down the relatively simple code we use for writing. Anyway,' Keilty continued, 'he can use both whenever he wants. In two years, Charlie has developed a large vocabulary and a fairly good grasp of abstracts for one who never even dreamed of their existence a short time before. I'd say this his general level of intelligence is about on a par with a twelve-year-old in abstract matters, and level with an intelligent full-grown man in most other things.'

Charlie had been fidgeting through Keilty's long dissertation and finally broke into the conversation, interrupting Redgrave who had been about to ask a question.

'What's up, doc?' Charlie's voice was a well-modulated imitation of Keilty's.

Both of the naval officers started and stared at each other. Charlie slid back part way and slapped the surface of the water with his tail.

Keilty looked pained. 'Cut out the funnies, Charlie, this is serious business. These gentlemen are here to ask our help. They have come to us because you are the only one that can do what they want, so quit clowning around.'

'Okay, sorry,' Charlie replied, still in a creditable imitation of Keilty's voice.

Jack bent over to pat his head. Keilty then explained briefly what they would need from Charlie and that it would give him a chance to ride in an airplane again. They would even put him by the window for the entire trip this time. Keilty did not explain why they needed the information, as it would only have confused the dolphin, or so he thought. He played up the airplane ride and the chance to see new territory.

The dolphin acquiesced easily enough, then demanded to know why.

'Oh brother, you *would* have to ask that.'

'Darned right. If you want me to go traipsing across the world, then you had better tell me why.'

'Look, Charlie,' Keilty said. 'I've tried to explain to you before about Communism as a political rather than economic system and our own . . .'

'Yeah, with that cornball analogy of the dolphins versus the sharks,' Charlie interrupted. 'What it all amounts to is that each of you wants the other of you to think and act the way he does, right?' Charlie finished smugly.

Keilty did a double take. 'Now how the devil did you arrive at that conclusion? I've been trying to pound just that idea into your thick head for nearly a year.'

'I've been sitting out on the reef thinking about it since last night's newscast. Eric Sevareid gave me the clue.'

'Eric Sevareid?' Keilty cried.

'Yep, he was talking about religion.'

'I give up.' Keilty threw up his hands. 'You see,' he said, turning to Rawingson, 'why the scientific method isn't much help here. Our own informal way sometimes works best. This is what I tried to convince those idiots of, back in Washington. But no – now everything has to be done by the book. Nuts!'

'All right,' he said, turning back to the dolphin, 'now that you have figured that out, are you convinced that we are right, or do you still maintain . . . ?'

'So are they convinced that they are right, apparently,' Charlie interrupted.

'So what? This is the side I live on,' Keilty shouted.

'Yeah. But that doesn't alter anything.'

Keilty sat back down beside the dolphin and scratched its leathery-hided head while the dolphin blinked in contentment like a sleek, bullet-shaped cat.

'I should know better than to argue philosophy with you,' he said accusingly. 'And so should you. We still have to build that frame of reference for abstractions, and you know it.'

The dolphin gave an almost human sigh and wriggled into a more comfortable position. Keilty dipped a bailing can full of water and poured it over the dolphin's exposed back.

'Hey, that feels good.'

Keilty continued to dip and pour. 'Still, you haven't explained to me why you want me to do all this for you.'

Keilty paused a moment, marshaling his thoughts. 'Remember a few weeks back when I explained to you about explosives?'

The dolphin thought for a moment, then brightened. He fastened his great eyes on Keilty. 'Yes I do. The expanding gases that tear things apart.'

'How about nuclear explosives?'

'What about them?'

'Well that's what my enemies intend to use. At sea, my friend. In the water. Boom. Dead fish all around. Poisoned water, et cetera.'

'The fish don't bother me,' Charlie said, rolling onto his left side for a better look at the two naval officers. 'Who are these cats?'

Keilty motioned the two slightly thunderstruck naval officers to approach.

'This one is Rear Admiral Peter Rawingson and this other is Lieutenant Commander Michael Redgrave. They are the people who need your help.'

Charlie regarded them for a moment, his eyes clouding slightly.

'Pardon my not shaking hands, but I'm not equipped for it as you can see.' He eyed Keilty again. 'Let me think about it. I'll let you know.'

Charlie slid back into the water, then poked his snout out. Keilty picked up the microphone lead. 'You said I can look out the window?'

'That's right, Charlie,' Keilty soberly answered him.

Charlie rose half out of the water for a long half a minute. Keilty could almost see the blood churning through his brain as the dolphin decided.

'All right then, I will.' He waited for Keilty to undo the microphone, then submerged.

Charlie dove towards the center of the pool and disappeared out into the lagoon.

Rawingson let out his breath in one short gust. 'That,' he stated, 'is the damnedest thing I have ever seen. That crazy fish sounded and acted human.'

'What's your definition of human, Admiral?' Jack asked, peering out towards the lagoon after the dolphin. 'He thinks, he rationalizes, and he is emotional. What else do you need to be human? A soul? What's that?' Jack turned towards the others, standing near the pool in the gathering dusk. The offshore breeze that always sprang up an hour before sunset had died away to nothing and the silence was nearly complete, broken only by the occasional call of an island bird. The sun had slipped beneath the western horizon to their backs and the light was fading fast in the brief tropical twilight. Already, in the east, single stars were glimmering fitfully. Jack shivered slightly and in a faraway voice said, 'You know, gentlemen, Mort here and I have argued for months about this. But I still maintain that Charlie and his race are the first real contact with an alien life form we've ever knowingly had. They are so completely different from us in mental processes that there is very little natural common ground. So don't be fooled by Charlie's apparent humanness. It's all learned.'

The darkness grew and silence held the four men until Margaritta, padding up quietly behind on bare feet, softly announced dinner.

CHAPTER THREE

The dolphin swam strongly out into the lagoon, troubled by the two strange men he had just met and the information Keilty had given him. He clearly recalled every word and intonation of the conversations concerning human relations that he had had with Keilty. He realized that Keilty was what humans called a rationalist. But beneath, and even more important, Keilty was an optimist. He had never clearly understood what optimism was until Jack had explained, using Keilty's relationship with Margaritta to put his point across. Even then, it had taken some time for him fully to grasp this totally human idea. The terms, or temperamental viewpoints of optimism, pessimism, and cynicism, etc., are related to the sense of time, since they are all concerned with what might happen tomorrow. Until Charlie had been taught by Keilty what tomorrow meant, he had never considered the concept of time. Dolphins had and needed no concept of time.

Yesterday, today, and tomorrow were needless, one and the same. There were no passing seasons to stimulate them in the sea; no need to build shelters. Their home was the sea and the sea furnished them both food and shelter. If food became scarce, they went somewhere else where food was more plentiful. They were born, lived, and died in the sea. They had no religion, because the sea supplied them with all they needed. Hence they had no need of a promised land or a better tomorrow, as all tomorrows were equally as good as today. The sea was bountiful. Keilty had once told Charlie that his race was either the most advanced or the most degenerate that he, Keilty, would ever encounter – and he was not sure which. Looking at it from Keilty's human standards, Charlie was not so sure either. But from the dolphin's point of view, he was sure that he was content – and probably degenerate, though the idea continued to bother him.

So Charlie had had to discover the idea of time. Jack suggested that he watch the sun and had given him a rudimentary counting system to use. Since that day, he had counted four hundred and seventy-three periods of alternating daylight and darkness. They still meant nothing to him, but he could see somewhat the importance of time to humans. Mentally, he gave the equivalent of a human shrug.

He was very much troubled by what Keilty had asked him to do. And, as he had lately found himself coming to do more and more when he had a problem, he filled his lungs and sounded for the base of the reef. The water was cool and dark some seventy feet down, and into one of the many empty overhangs, he could insert his body to satisfy his survival instincts. Any enemies had to approach from the front. He wriggled his bulk in and relaxed to think through the problem. First of all, before meeting Keilty he had never had a problem in his life. Dolphins lived by the old axiom 'all things come to him who waits' – without realizing it. Then, he had learned that in the world of humans there were such things as problems.

He had decided on the spur of the moment to involve himself in a human problem. He had always been reluctant to do this before. He stayed near Keilty because he was as curious as Keilty was. But now, why all of a sudden had he said yes? He had insufficient data to go on and basically he could see no real differences in the two opposing sides. He did not understand the ideologies or ramifications involved for humans, and he sensed that it would be better if he did not. His own kind were satisfied with their few problems and certainly did not wish for human problems. Degeneracy again, he decided.

Perhaps it was Keilty – there was a compatibility between them that he did not recognize as friendship since that concept was alien also. He considered Keilty to be one of the herd in which he grew up – a part of the family so to speak. Keilty now wanted his help. If he did help, it would make Keilty happy. He recognized that he had never been dependent on Keilty the way humans were dependent on each other. Margaritta again – or was it Keilty? He had never been held captive, nor did Keilty feed him. He was free to come and go, and he did as it pleased him, and Keilty had never interfered.

Charlie was faced with a dilemma – not of deciding whether or not he would help, because he had already told Keilty he would – but of resolving his own conflict: to become involved in a human problem.

He could see the problems in taking sides with either faction, could see the factions factionating down through a series of images to infinity, as if in parallel mirrors.

His justification of the course he had taken was honestly rationalized – mostly because, lacking the distinction between honesty and dishonesty, he chose this course because he wanted to help. And because he was rather curious. And now that he thought about it, he realized that Keilty had played on the right chord in offering him a chance to watch out the window of the airplane. He had flown once before and had been completely captivated by the process of flying. Another chance was too good to pass up. Perhaps he was not so honest after all, he decided. Then it came to him that he had a better understanding of honesty than Keilty thought he did, or himself for that matter. It troubled him a little that perhaps he was becoming a bit too human.

CHAPTER FOUR

Cold tropical rain pounded the decks and upper works of the H.M.S. *Bradley*, wallowing heavily in the stormy waters of the Strait of Malacca.

'Meteorological report says the rain will last another twenty-five minutes, sir.' The rain-slickered executive officer recapped the speaking tube and turned to the captain.

'You chaps about ready?'

Keilty nodded to Rawingson. 'We're about set, Admiral. Captain, can you swing this pogo stick into the wind when I give the signal, then cut your engines long enough for Charlie to get away?'

'Yes, I think so. Wouldn't do to cut up our spy, now would it?'

Keilty swung down the ladder, muttering to himself. Charlie was ensconced in his tank, fastened to the starboard bow just inside the railing, and looking very unhappy.

Keilty flipped on the transphonemator.

'This damned stuff chafes,' was the first thing Charlie said. He didn't understand the deeper meanings of profanity but agreed with Keilty that for emphasis, it had no substitute.

'Knock off the griping, I gave you your chance when we were fitting it out,' Keilty growled humorously.

'Maybe, but there's a big difference between just trying this junk on and actually wearing it.' The dolphin was loaded around his shoulders with equipment to power and control the two TV cameras mounted on either side of his head to give a stereo effect. They were encased in watertight rectangular and contoured plastic kits 18″ × 20″ × 3″. The equipment was slung around his shoulders in two pocketed belts that resembled oversized cartridge belts. A flexible metal strip ran the length of his back from shoulders to tail to serve as an antenna.

Keilty peered over the spray-lashed side of the destroyer and came back to the tank. 'It looks pretty rough down there. Do you think you can get into the water without any trouble?'

Charlie peered at the series of mirrors, shielded from the rain, that angled over the side to give him a view of what was below. 'Really kicking up a storm down there, isn't it?' He contemplated for a moment. 'When you're ready, drain the water out of the tank first. I don't want it twisting me around. Swing the board over and then dump. And for God's sake, warn me first. That's a long way down.'

'All right, we're ready,' Keilty shouted towards the bridge, and waved an arm. Then he pulled out the stops in the bottom that drained the tank.

Charlie grunted as the supporting water ran out and he settled into a rather flaccid heap. With the help of two British sailors, Keilty wheeled the tank over to the railing, then pulled away the sides. Charlie now lay poised on a swivel board, half over the rail. With the microphones and tape recorders unplugged, Keilty was unable to understand Charlie's high-pitched squeaks of complaint. He waited, grinning into the mirrors and stroking the dolphin's flank to calm him, judging the depth of the waves. A few seconds later, the destroyer buried its bow in a deep wave that washed solid spray over them. The following wave was the one he had been waiting for. It built under the bow, lifting the ship over its crest, then slid past as the bow sliced down, cleaving the water into a churning furrow, down into the trough. As they crested again, Keilty waved his arm vigorously to port and the helmsman on the bridge peering at him through the revolving screen, turned the destroyer into the beginning of an S-curve. The bow plowed through the furrow into the next wave and Keilty slapped Charlie on the side and upended the board. The dolphin gave a powerful kick with his tail and shot clear in a long curving arc that carried him away from the destroyer's side. He disappeared into the boiling green water less than six feet below with hardly a splash, and sounded desperately.

The helmsman swung the helm back, slewing away from the spot where Charlie had disappeared and bringing the thrashing propellers clear of the furiously swimming dolphin.

The fast-swinging bow smashed into another wave, just below the crest, and the destroyer rattled and shook along its stern as tons of sea water smothered the bow. Without their life lines, Keilty and the two sailors would have been swept overboard. As it was, they were nearly drowned as the water flung them around like corks before it cascaded off the decks. Breathing heavily, the three pushed to the rail, but there was no sign of the dolphin in the churning leaden-green waters below.

Keilty straightened up from where he had been leaning over the rail and glanced at the two ratings. 'Thanks, fellows,' he said briefly, grinning at both, and made his way across the heaving deck and up onto the bridge. Halfway up the ladder, he frowned, suddenly apprehensive about what he had done.

Charlie swam strongly below the turbulent wake created by the ship. Five minutes out from his point of entry, he began swimming aimlessly, as Keilty had instructed him to do. If the research station had spotted the ship, they would surely be listening on sonar for more underwater trespassers, and would have spotted the dolphin leaving the ship. From there, his cover would be good if he could find and blend in with a school of good-sized fish. Keilty had once explained to Charlie how sonar worked, but Charlie had been way ahead of him – had in fact been amazed at the limitations of the human device.

After what he judged was sufficient time, he began swimming in the general direction of the Vietnamese research station. By now, he had gotten out of the storm area that had carried on north on the prevailing winds. The sun was shining strongly enough on the surface to light quite clearly the thirty-foot or so depth at which he was swimming. The water tasted and smelled different to Charlie. This was the first time he had ever been away from the waters that he knew around the Keys. He was not afraid, since fear was an alien abstraction to him. What he felt was more an extension or a heightening of his senses that put him on edge, made him doubly alert – a feeling he had felt before when his few natural enemies were in the neighborhood: sharks, and once a killer whale that he had identified from the descriptions once given him by his master. He was nervous, but since this feeling had never been described to him by humans, he did not recognize it as a human feeling.

Charlie swam on, from time to time noticing strange fish with which he was not acquainted. Other than that, it seemed to him much like swimming in the open ocean at home. The water was delightfully warm and he swam happily, beginning to lose his nervousness as he became used to the new surroundings. About an hour after leaving the ship, he began to pick up the scent of man and seconds later his own variety of sonar showed a large bulky object, or series of bulky objects, dead ahead.

As he swam closer, he began to make out the image of some type of strandlike obstruction reaching to near the surface. When he sounded for air, he was only some ten feet from the buoyed net. He swam up and nudged it playfully. Nothing happened. The bright yellow buoys fastened all along the top bobbed erratically, but the net remained in place. Keilty had described netting to him and told him he could expect to run into some type of it. Charlie swam back and forth along the netting for a ways, then sounded, swimming down along the net to see how deep it went. The mesh was quite fine, about half an inch wide, and beyond he could now see what was another, thicker net made of steel cables.

Charlie swam back to the surface to consider for a moment. He picked up the sound of a boat's propellers moving through the water quite fast. Above him, the mirror image of the underside of the surface was broken quite suddenly by a V-shaped trail and a turbulent wake as a twenty-foot patrol boat passed over him.

Charlie swam quickly to the surface, careful to keep the equipment strapped to him out of sight as much as possible. He was beginning to think this was all rather ridiculous and not in keeping with his fine sense of dolphin propriety, but Keilty had warned him to be careful.

He chased after the patrol boat, slapped the surface with his tail to attract their attention, then showed his dorsal fin. The boat rounded on him in a sweeping turn and came back under full power. Charlie dived and stayed below the surface out of their sight. Apparently they were satisfied that it was only a fish that had disturbed the net, as they roared off towards the research station barely visible in the humid mist. Charlie listened to the sound of the propellers disappearing in the distance, then swam back to the net. He was careful not to touch it this time.

When the net was before him, he cruised slowly along, ascending at the same time until he was again at the surface. The top of the net was flush with the surface and there was about twice his length between it and the next fence, which, according to what Keilty had told him, was presumably charged. He considered the distance, then backed off and shot forward into the air over both nets at once. He caused a loud smack as he splashed back into the water, but surfacing again to look around, he could not see that it had tripped any alarms or alerted anyone. He wondered briefly what alarms were as he cruised around the surface, waiting to see if anything would happen now. Keilty had said that he should avoid alarms but had neglected to tell him what they were.

With his beak out of the water, he cleared his lungs through his blowhole, then refilled them to capacity with fresh air. Sighting on the station lying across the oily sea from him in the tropical afternoon, he sounded as deeply as he dared, and swam forward. He was not too sure of the distance because, out of the water, appearances were still deceptive to him, but he surged forward at close to twenty-five knots.

Shortly, a long thick column that he had spotted with his sonar, minutes before, appeared in front of him, and he braked with his tail and surfaced carefully.

The Vietnamese had obviously made no attempt to hide the presence of the tower. The main platform reared nearly sixty feet above the choppy waves and rested on a series of concrete and steel pillars, which Charlie could see were mounted on concrete caissons sunk deep into the sea floor. The platform itself was triangular in shape and supported the main derrick, which rose another one hundred and twenty feet. A large revolving aircraft strobe light was mounted on the top of the derrick, which was painted fluorescent yellow. Two smaller cranes were stationed at the midpoints of two of the equilateral sides. Two housing structures, one of them extending the width of the base, took up two thirds of the deck. The building at the apex of the triangle supported a helicopter landing pad, while the largest building provided space for air conditioning machinery, pipe racks, and equipment storage. The deck itself was twenty feet thick and contained living and working areas.

A small, heavily guarded boat stage was attached to the forward main support. One small powerboat was tied up at the moment, while the guards smoked and lounged in what little shade was provided by the deck. Charlie could see a narrow ladder mounted between the two buildings and reaching the top of the deck near the drilling rig. Several black oil drums were clustered at the top.

Small groups of men were working near the derrick, but other than that, the deck was deserted. He caught the sound of one of the patrol boats approaching, and taking another deep breath, he submerged carefully and moved forward.

The water seemed to be quite thick and was full of refuse that hampered his vision. He swam between the columns, around a second and a third, until he emerged on the other side. Turning to his left, he swam out of the refuse-laden water and switched on his cameras. Immediately, he received a pulse close to his ear that told him the humans were aware that he had activated his equipment. He swam slowly forward until a large pillar again appeared. The water was much heavier here, with a nauseating taste to it, and the current so slow that he was barely able to detect it. He was directly in front of the pillar, some forty feet away. He could see practically nothing visually, but his sonar defined everything sharply for several hundred yards in every direction. Satisfied, he waited for the double pulse that would mean that Keilty was seeing what he saw. It did not come. Puzzled, he swam closer, cutting the distance in half. He could just make out the hazy image of the tower substructure with his eyes, but still no pulse. When he was less than ten feet away, the pulse came suddenly. They must be blind back there, he muttered to himself.

Now he began to swim even more slowly, letting himself rise up the pillar until he nudged something above him. He backed away to investigate and saw that it was some kind of barnacle-encrusted shelf. Then he saw that the pillar fitted neatly into the center of the shelf. Something shiny attracted his attention to the leg of the tower and he moved over to investigate. As he watched, a glistening drop broke away and formed a bubble, which shot towards the surface. When the next one detached itself, he snapped at it with his beak and immediately his mouth filled with a thick cloying taste that burned. Violently, he expelled all the stored air in his lungs and rushed for the surface. He broke the surface in a jump that carried him half out of the water. He drew in deep draughts of water, sloshing it from side to side until he was able to clear some of the taste from his mouth. The burning was not quite so bad now and he lay quietly on the surface, shuddering through his entire length, fighting to regain his breath. Though he did not know it, what he had tasted was a much higher concentration of the substance in the water around him – lubricating oil to keep sea life from encrusting the retractable legs of the sea tower.

Three quick pulses were repeated over and over. Keilty was sending a query, puzzled as to why the transmission had broken off. Charlie pulled himself together, and began swimming slowly. It was quite dark where he was, although a ring of bright sunlight showed all around. He deduced that he was under whatever the pillars were holding up. Off to his right, a long shaft – sunk straight down into the water – blocked the light from a small segment of the circle. Charlie swam to it, and taking a deep breath, he began to swim down the column hesitatingly. The pulses came again to show that Keilty was interested in what he saw. The shaft was quite a bit thicker than the others and was formed of segments rather than being one continuous column. It ended forty feet below the surface in a large bulbous structure some twenty feet across that looked like a flattened rubber ball.

There was a large hatch, which he investigated, making sure that the camera picked up a good image of the hatch and its opening mechanism. He swam around the structure and then under it. Beneath was a heavy steel plate that flared upward, supplementing the spheroidal steel structure. This steel plating was featureless, without even rivet holes, which would have been meaningless to Charlie anyway.

The dolphin bumped at it with his nose, smelling the steel, but not tasting it. He had learned his lesson. He became aware of the chafing of the equipment belts around his shoulders in the form of a violent itch. To scratch it, he tried to rub his back against the plating. Suddenly, his ears were filled with an insistent chattering. At the same time, Keilty began sending excited pulses to tell him to stay where he was. Charlie held motionless, his back bumping against the plating while the chattering continued. Keilty pulsed the code that indicated to him that he was to swim slowly forward. As he did so, the chattering lessened in frequency.

He backed and turned in obedience to the pulses until Keilty had him swimming slowly beneath and almost touching the flattened sphere. The chattering was continuous now.

After about fifteen minutes, Keilty directed him to get what pictures he could from beneath the structure. By the time Charlie had finished, the sun was halfway below the horizon. In response to Keilty's signals, he surfaced cautiously some five hundred yards from the tower structure.

The red sun painted the white steel tower golden in the dwindling twilight, licking drops of quicksilver from the long swells pushing up the strait. Charlie paused to breathe and then began swimming slowly towards the structure in a circling maneuver. The main deck of the tower was clearly lighted against the deepening blue of the eastern horizon. Lights were appearing on the tower and the superstructure of the drilling rig. The monotonous clanking of the drilling machinery served to cover the faint noises the dolphin made as he swam to within fifty feet of the tower and began to circle it.

The figure of a man appeared briefly near the railing, clearly outlined against the sky. He fumbled briefly with something near the railing and Charlie sounded, startled as floodlights bathed the area around the tower. Charlie's thoughts were strictly dolphinic as he rose again to the surface, this time staying completely underwater, except to breathe. He began to swim away from the lighted area, until the shadows were deep enough to surface. By now he was some eight hundred feet away from the station. He took a good look, letting the cameras pan over the scene. The tower was too far away to detect details, and his sonar told him that there were several surface craft making random search patterns around the station.

He let himself settle again until he was about twenty feet below the surface, and began extending his sonar field. His maximum sonar range was ten miles or so, although he was not aware of the distance in human terms.

The station commanded most of his field to the east, and to the west he could just barely make out the dim echo of the *Bradley*. The sharply defined echoes and subechoes from the station said 'human' to Charlie, as they were sharp but vibrating at the same time. He concentrated on the station, laying out its underwater pattern until he was sure where every underwater leg and support was. Then he began to examine the area around the tower – the island rising beyond, the slope of the channel bottom to the island shore. Except for the crosscurrents which he could detect, the picture was relatively uninteresting: volcanic sand bottom with a profusion of marine growth.

Charlie narrowed his sonar beam until it was pulsing outward in a forty-five-degree arc, and started sweeping around in a circle.

A clearer, tighter picture built up: the island sloping away into a narrow channel, the bases of several more distant islands showing, and schools of unfamiliar fish. Charlie pivoted slowly on until the beam was fanning an open area of channel between two islands that led away to the South China Sea.

A reflection appeared. At first Charlie thought it was a whale. Then he noticed it was resting on the bottom. The object was near the limit of his sonar's capability. Keilty had said to get back as fast as possible, so he could not waste any time for a closer look. He waited, sorting out the multiplicity of reflections until he isolated the one he wanted. There, shimmering near the limits of his awareness, was the peculiar echo and subecho of metal. Charlie was puzzled. The object seemed to be resting less than a mile from the base of a large island. He watched it for a while, examining the blurred image as best he could until he had it as sharply defined as possible. Suddenly he remembered. He had seen a submarine once before in his home waters, and had chased it for miles, watchings its strange antics as it maneuvered around several surface ships in the area.

His curiosity satisfied, he completed his sonar sweep and surfaced for a last look around. The sun had set and darkness had swiftly blanketed the area. He could see nothing of the tower now but the lights in the rigging and the floodlit expanse of water all around.

He wondered again about the submarine and its presence near the base of the island, then forgot about it as a wide beam of light, mounted on the drilling rig, began to sweep the water beyond the limits of the floodlights. He watched the distended oval of light ripple across the water to him, and taking a breath, settled slowly. Seconds later, it passed over him, creating a pattern of tangled silver on the mirrorlike underside of the surface. They were certainly being careful, he thought, then turned away and swam strongly for the netting.

A few minutes later, he surfaced again only twenty feet from the net. Complete darkness had fallen by now, and turning, he could see the bright ring of floodlights glowing like a broad band of fire on the surface. Above was the flickering searchlight, with the aircraft warning lights dangling below.

He had done as Keilty had asked him to. Keilty had explained about the Geiger counter before they left the Keys. The fact that it had worked – the loud clicking – meant they had found the bomb. Now, he wondered, what was the next step?

He thought he knew enough about humans to guess. The bomb posed a threat to one side – Keilty's side. But it was the upper hand for the other side. That meant that Keilty's side would have to go and take it away. In the process, a lot of people could get killed. That last fact meant little to him, no more than if he were a human and knew that several dolphins might be killed if, say, sharks attacked. If you could find enough foolhardy sharks, he thought seriously.

So long as Keilty was not killed, the death of a human meant little to him, because beyond Jack, Margaritta, Keilty, and now Rawingson, he knew very little of humans. And, he suspected, he knew little – important data, that is – about the four he did know.

The fact that he had found the bomb meant that he had now taken sides in human affairs. Something he had wondered about

– and had halfway decided not to do – ever since he had started watching the TV set Keilty had installed in his pen.

He thought to himself, without humor, that he had come to the point were he was studying humans, as much as Keilty was studying his people. Who had the upper edge here: Keilty, because he was a trained observer, or himself, because the television and the microfilmed books gave him – with his totally fresh viewpoint – a greater insight into the mind of humans, a mind which he was coming more and more to discover was not only a product of the particular society in which a man lived, but in addition, contrary to the widespread human concept, did little to shape an individual's relations with other humans?

As Keilty had once told him, a human was a totally selfish animal. He loved because he liked the feeling. He helped someone in need because it made him feel good. He was patriotic because it satisfied what was left of his almost atrophied herd instincts. Charlie took this one step further. Man did not live on a rational level, but on an emotional level. Charlie's people, on the other hand, more closely approached the rational level, and he was discovering, in reviewing his past life now that he had the mental tool – vocabulary – to work with, that in the dolphin, emotions were almost atrophied and the herd worked and existed together on a rational level.

Now that he was discovering the effects of emotions, he was beginning to realize just how strong they could be.

Not far away, the silence was shattered by the passage of a patrol boat touring the net perimeter. Startled, he dove, suddenly aware of the dangers to which he had left himself open. He executed a fast 360° turn, sonar and hearing tuned to the sharpest possible degree. The images were familiar: the tower; odd schools of fish, nothing big; the patrol boat; and dimly, the *Bradley*. The submarine was completely out of range now.

He watched the patrol boat, and as soon as it was far enough away, he cleared the nets in one jump and headed quickly back to the *Bradley*.

CHAPTER FIVE

The lights went up in the crowded wardroom, highlighting the wreaths of cigarette and pipe smoke coiling suddenly in the steaming air. Keilty sat to one side of the long captain's table, silently listening to the quiet arguing of the gathered officers and civilians.

Keilty's contempt for the military and civil service mind had never been stronger. They had been sitting for hours in the crowded wardroom, all through the hot, sticky late afternoon, debating the pros and cons of the information that Charlie had brought back. It was all there for them to see, but some remained stubbornly unconvinced. Sitting next to him, almost wilting in the heat, was a slight, balding man. He drummed nervously on a small sheaf of papers until they were almost unreadable – the penciled calculations were smeared and blurred with perspiration.

Keilty had been on deck earlier in the evening, shortly after Charlie had returned, when the MTB had come sliding up alongside the *Bradley*. Lines were secured as he slouched on the railing watching. The American secretaries of State and Defense, the British Foreign Secretary and Minister of War, and their Australian, Malaysian, New Zealand and Indonesian counterparts, and respective retinues came aboard the destroyer. The seas were beginning to pick up and the ship was rolling heavily in the increasing swells. They had gone below, some of them already green, and a few moments later a messenger had come for him. Keilty finished his cigarette and went below. They were waiting for him, impatiently, and with a barrage of questions.

He produced an extremely black Connecticut-broadleaf-wrappered and foul-smelling cigar, and lit up. Puffing on it with relish, he began to answer questions. The small wardroom soon filled with the cloying stench but the questions went on and on. Finally Keilty had to admit defeat. The smoke was getting to him as well. As unobtrusively as possible, he extinguished the cigar and covered it with an empty paper cup. Later, the tapes were produced and he narrated the now-familiar scenes as Charlie approached the station, examined the structure and support columns, the blur of motion as he surfaced and tried to rinse the taste of the oil from his mouth, and the underwater shots of the bomb housing.

The silence was nearly complete when he finished, broken only by the whirring of the overworked and totally ineffective air conditioner.

'There, gentlemen, you have it. It's as plain as the warts on a hog what is going on. What's to be done is now your bailiwick.' And he sat down.

As the argument renewed and dragged on, he talked quietly with the balding man next to him. It turned out that he was Dr. Iver Jensen, a Pentagon expert on the effects of nuclear weapons. So far, he had not been asked to speak.

Keilty turned his attention to the discussion. Some Australian official was pooh-poohing the idea first of all, that there was a bomb, and secondly, that the subsequent detonation of said nonexistent bomb could do the damage expected. He was supported by several others, notably the Americans. The Malaysians were looking extremely worried. Keilty glanced across the wardroom at Rawingson's set expression and decided it was time to do something.

He stood up and whistled. The piercing scream of the whistle echoed in the steel-walled wardroom, overriding even the nasal tones of a loud-mouthed American general who turned surprised and angry eyes on Keilty. Keilty paid no attention. He had disliked this man ever since he had seen him on television years before, defending a particularly obnoxious right-wing group.

The American Secretary of State turned and peered at him through his steel-rimmed glasses. 'You have something to contribute, Dr. Keilty?'

'Nope, but Dr. Jensen does. Why don't you all shut up and listen to him for a while. You fatheads are not making much sense anyway.'

Admiral Rawingson, grinning widely, told a junior officer to shut up and sit down, then settled back comfortably and waited.

'Some of you here,' Keilty continued, unabashed at the angry mutterings, 'know who Dr. Jensen is – you explain to the guy next to you if he doesn't. Dr. Jensen?' Keilty indicated the audience and the speaker's position.

Jensen stood up, all traces of his nervousness disappearing quickly as he adopted his favourite speaking attitude and launched into his speech.

'Gentlemen, we have beyond a certainty established that the Vietnamese have now manufactured, not one, but several nuclear bombs. There is no reason to doubt that fact any longer. At the latest count, there are some fourteen nations with nuclear weapons. Now, thanks to Dr. Keilty's dolphin, we know where at least one of these bombs is. It is sitting not twenty-five miles from us, forty-five feet below the surface of the entrance to the Strait of Malacca.'

He waited until the angry murmuring from both sides of contention died away somewhat.

'Whatever you believe at the moment is of no importance. There can be no doubt about it. That bomb is there. The radiation readings are too strong to be anything but those from a crude fusion device, poorly shielded . . .' Jensen raised his hand to forestall a question. 'No, the radiation is much too strong to come from drilling or current-tracing processes.'

Jensen pulled the tripod-mounted blackboard around and quickly sketched the outline of the strait – essentially a narrow channel running southeast to northwest and widening gradually at the two-hundred-mile point until it was nearly two hundred miles wide at the five-hundred-mile extreme length. At the entrance to the strait, he drew in the island of Singapore and the Malay Peninsula, and directly south, dotted a group of islands that filled the entrance, leaving only narrow channels. With a series of dots he indicated the major concentration of the various fleets in and around the strait. To the south, he drew the ragged outline of the coast of Sumatra and its islanded shore.

'Now, gentlemen,' he went on, turning to face the others, 'you are all pretty much familiar with this area by now. As you can see, the Vietnamese research station and the bomb – are here in the center of these islands at the head of the strait. These islands are volcanic in origin and their peaks are quite lofty, rising some eight and nine thousand feet. These two islands are our two *containment* islands. By that, I mean that these two islands will absorb a good portion of the blast and shock wave, thereby protecting the two mainlands from bomb damage *per se*. The smaller islands forming the apex of the triangle will seal off the South China Sea from both the bomb blast and the resulting tidal wave. Now, because the wind currents in this area are northerly, and quite strong at high altitudes, the majority of fallout in the form of radioactive rain will be carried north across Singapore and southern Malaya state.

'The channel of the Malaccan strait is four to five hundred miles long – only two hundred of which are important to us. These two hundred miles are the narrows, the area where guerrilla infiltration is the heaviest and where the Malaysian and Indonesian patrols are concentrated. I don't think anyone here will dispute the fact that it is only the presence of these fleets that prevents a major infiltration south into Sumatra as well as north into the southerly portions of Malaya.' Jensen beamed around the room. 'As you remember, prior to the Communist coup which failed a few years ago, the Indonesians were ready to mount an all-out offensive on both the Malay Peninsula and the Malaysian-held half of Borneo. A foothold in Sumatra would be an extreme danger to both nations.

'But, to continue, the strait is relatively shallow – roughly twenty-five fathoms – and only about thirty miles wide.

'If, gentlemen, this five-megaton bomb is exploded in its present location, a tidal wave will sweep up this channel, carrying everything with it to destruction. If you don't believe me, and I see a great number of you don't, it can be proven with a few simple calculations. Permit me?

'The shallow underwater bursts,' Jensen said, juggling the stub of chalk, 'of the Bikini "Baker" tests in the late 1940s, give us a set of data from which we may extrapolate. Our problem is first to determine pressure variance between open-water explosions and open-channel – such as the strait – explosions at equal distances. We do this as the Bikini tests were conducted in open water, and therefore, the data we have is based on open-water explosions.

'If we assume a radius of one hundred miles for easy calculation, and draw a rough sketch of the blast area:

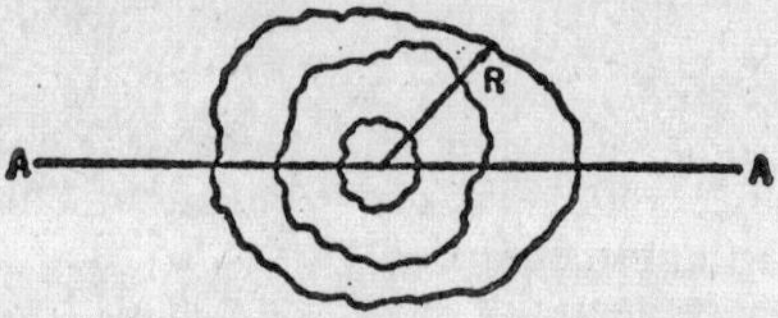

we can find the amount of water moved above the line A–A by the simple relationship: Q equals AV, where Q is the flowrate (in miles 3/hr. in this case), A is the area of the wavefront at a distance which I'll call R, and V is the speed at which the wavefront is moving. If we put them all together in an equation and solve it, we get:

$$Q = \tfrac{1}{2}(2\pi R)V$$
$$= \pi RV$$
$$= 100\pi V$$

assuming, of course, that depth equals unity.

'Now, if we picture the Strait of Malacca as looking like this:

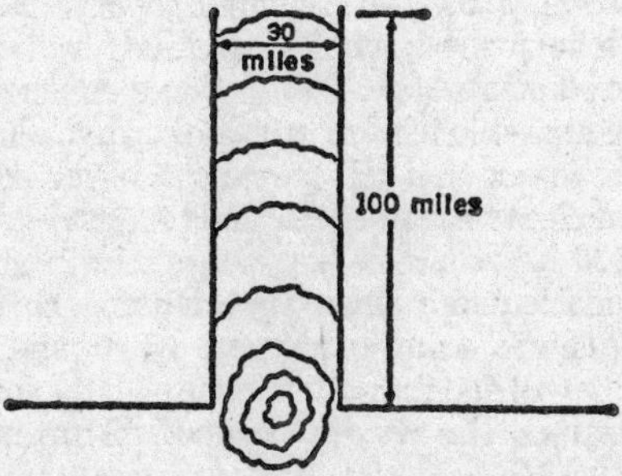

we can assume that the arc length of the wavefront at one hundred miles will be just a bit greater than thirty miles; say, closer to forty, since any wave produced will overlap the land. If so, once again we can find the amount of water moved, but in this case, just the amount up the strait, by using the relationship Q=AV again, but adding in the forty-mile wavefront, like this:

$$Q = AV$$
$$= 40V$$

again assuming that depth equals unity.

'Now, let's examine this a little. Assuming that there are no flow losses nor any areas where pressures will be equal – equal point pressures, in other words – the amount of water moved by an exploding bomb in the open sea will equal the amount of water moved in a closed channel. Or:

$$100\pi V_{open} = 40V_{closed}$$
$$\frac{V_{closed}}{V_{open}} = \frac{100\pi}{40}$$
$$= 7.85$$

'Now, apply Bernoulli's principle: pressure is proportional to the square of the velocity. Or in this case, we find that the pressure will be sixty-one and sixty-two hundredths times greater in the channel than in the open sea.

'In other words, gentlemen, this all means that the velocity of water moved up that channel will be seven point eighty-five times *faster* than it would be in the open sea, and further, the pressure behind that wavefront of moving water will be sixty-one point sixty-two times *greater* in that channel than in the open sea.'

Jensen paused in his whirlwind delivery. 'Stick with me, gentlemen, we've just begun. And we haven't even come to the bomb yet,' he said with a grin.

Keilty craned closer for a better look. The calculations were just so much Greek to him. He was a psychologist and had flunked second-year high-school algebra while a freshman in college.

'Do you gentlemen realize the significance of these two equations. They are going to cause a wave, and quite a wave at that, as you will see in a moment. But let's go on. Based on constants used in the Kutter-Ganquillet formula for open-channel flow:

$$N = 0{\cdot}010 \text{ for a smooth surface}$$
$$N = 0{\cdot}050 \text{ for a natural channel}$$

we can state that the pressure change in the channel will be only one fifth of what we calculated just now, since we have been assuming that the strait's channel had a smooth bottom. So now we have:

$$\begin{aligned} \triangle P &= 61{\cdot}62/5 \\ &= 12{\cdot}32 \end{aligned}$$

and because of the bad sea conditions expected tomorrow as well as pressure absorption out into the open sea, we shall assume a maximum dispersion of four and still get:

$$\begin{aligned} \triangle P &= 12{\cdot}32/4 \\ &= 3{\cdot}08 \end{aligned}$$

which simply indicates that any bomb exploded in a thirty-mile-wide channel would effect a water-pressure force equivalent to that produced by a bomb at least three times its size, exploded in open water.'

Jensen paused again, this time waiting for the conclusions to sink in. Keilty, who had only a layman's hazy idea of the sizes and potential power of thermonuclear weapons, was puzzled at the deeply shocked silence and then the flurry of activity that followed. Common sense told him that any bomb exploded in a confined area would do more damage than one exploded in open surroundings. He did not realize, however, the magnitude, size, and power involved. Slide rules were hurriedly consulted and notes and equations began to fill scratch pads, but Jensen did not wait. He went on at breakneck speed.

'Now, gentlemen, comes the real corker. We know that a five-megaton bomb will be equivalent to a fifteen-megaton bomb in this situation, a seven to a twenty-one, ten to thirty, twelve to thirty-six, fifteen to a forty-five, et cetera. We can extrapolate from a simple chart; I believe it is figure six point seven nine from the *Effects of Nuclear Weapons*, an Atomic Energy Commission publication – I forgot to write it down earlier,' he admitted somewhat sheepishly. 'Anyway, figuring our five-megaton bomb to equal fifteen megatons – which is fifteen thousand kilotons for ease in calculation – we can easily extrapolate from known graphs.

'Since the chart is scaled to eighty-five feet, we must rescale the graph:

$$\text{Scale height} = 180/(15{,}000)^{1/4} = 16{\cdot}26 \text{ ft.}$$

According to this graph, the scale factor will be:

$$\text{Scale factor} = {\cdot}036(16{\cdot}26) = {\cdot}585$$

and the resultant wave height:

$$\text{Wave height} = {\cdot}585(15{,}000)^{1/2} = 71{\cdot}7 \text{ ft.}$$

All of which gives us a wave that even at the two-hundred-mile mark from surface zero will be seventy-one feet high for a five-megaton bomb. The wave height from this bomb at thirty miles from surface zero can be derived:

$$\text{Scale factor} = {\cdot}18(16{\cdot}26) = 2{\cdot}93 \text{ ft.}$$

Again the wave height would be:

$$\text{Wave height} = 2{\cdot}93(15{,}000)^{1/2} = 370 \text{ ft.}$$

which means that this wave will be three hundred and seventy feet high thirty miles from the explosion site or surface zero!'

By now, the gathered military and government officials had received so many shocks that they merely greeted the result that they had all been afraid to admit was the only answer, with silence.

'A last thought, gentlemen,' Jensen said, rubbing off the blackboard. He turned to face the assembled wardroom. 'The force of this wave along its thirty- to forty-mile-wide front will be on the order of one hundred billion pounds! The coast of Malaya bordering on the strait is low-lying flatlands, while the coast of Sumatra is fairly high, shading up to coastal mountain ranges. A wave of this size and with this much power behind it in a channel as narrow as Malacca will most surely be a breaker type of wave, and not a long swell.

'If you are at all familiar with tidal waves, you know that no matter how great the wave or the force it packs, it is a long swell in the open ocean over which ships ride, hardly knowing they have been caught in a tidal wave. However, when these tidal waves approach shallows and bays or harbors, they become immense breakers. That is the situation we face here.'

Jensen turned quickly to the commander of the *Bradley*, 'Captain, would you say that you could ride out a fifty-foot wave – a breaker wave – let alone a three-hundred-and-seventy-foot breaker?'

'Well, I don't know,' the captain answered slowly. 'A fifty-foot breaker maybe. But any ship smaller than ours would not stand a chance.'

'Exactly, sir, anything smaller would not stand a chance against a wave of this size. And most of your fleet is composed of motor torpedo boats, corvettes, and small minesweepers – and destroyers such as yourselves. Thank you, gentlemen.' And he sat down. A complete and dead silence answered the end of Jensen's lecture.

From where he sat, Keilty spoke up again. 'How about that? With one fell swoop, the Vietnamese are going to wipe out not only your naval squadrons but shore-based installations as well. With the Malaysian armed forces disorganized and in retreat up the peninsula or engaged in rescue work, the Australians, New Zealanders and the Indonesians helpless because of their parliaments and their own lack of naval craft, the insurgents backed by the Vietnamese are going to come down that peninsula and beat the hell out of whoever is left.'

His voice was heavy with sarcasm as he went on. 'They will close the world's busiest shipping lanes to whoever they want and scare the hell out of the Philippines, Japan, India, Thailand, et cetera.

'That bomb will kill thousands of your troops and sailors, wreak havoc with the Indonesian fleet in the strait and the

Australasian fleet in Singapore and throw you all the hell out of the Indo-China peninsula.'

Keilty's voice was calm but his face was angry and red. Everyone in the steaming wardroom was quiet, listening to him expound the fears they were loath to admit.

'Perhaps you will bomb,' he continued, his voice beginning to rise. 'The U.S. won't be able to give you much help. We are overextended in this area now since Congress' cutback last year.

'What will you do?' he challenged the British Foreign Secretary. 'Use nuclear bombs on Vietnam? Invade? Not likely. It's been tried before.

'Can't you people realize that this is big, not just an isolated incident, but part of a well-planned scheme to kick you people all the hell out of this part of the world. You don't play around with nuclear weapons for kicks, and they know it as well as you.'

'Face it,' Keilty's voice was very cold, 'they have you if that bomb goes off.' He paused for a moment, then went on, 'Your problem is to see that that bomb does not go off. It's as simple as that.'

There was silence for a moment when he finished speaking. Finally, the British Foreign Secretary spoke. 'Thank you, Dr. Keilty. We are well aware of the problems we face here. However, there are certain ramifications, such as incursion on a sovereign nation's territory, world opinion . . .'

'Nuts,' Keilty interrupted shortly. 'World opinion be damned. You and the French let yourselves be swayed by world opinion in fifty-six, and as a result, Nasser made laughing stocks out of you.'

The American Secretary of Defense coughed and fidgeted. Keilty grinned.

'This time,' he went on, 'you are going to make asses out of yourselves if you continue to sit around down here and let that bomb go off. As for world opinion, the Vietnamese have dug themselves their own grave. This research station has received a fair amount of publicity in the past few months. So turn it against them. Pull a surprise raid and disarm the bomb before they can set it off.'

A signalman came in hurriedly, saluted, and handed a flimsy to the H.M.S. *Bradley*'s captain. He read it through and looked up solemnly.

'Gentlemen, there seems to be a Vietnamese warship on

course for the station. Satellite reports indicate that she left Saigon earlier today. Our intelligence believes the ship to be a destroyer delivering the trigger device and that it will take the people off the research station. Their estimated time of arrival is nine hundred hours tomorrow.'

'And,' Keilty interrupted, 'you have a heavily armed destroyer, a hundred marines, and two MTBs. And your last chance.' He stood up abruptly and went on deck, pausing to speak briefly with Charlie in his tank near the bow where they were preparing to take him below. After a few minutes he left and climbed forward over the winch until he was leaning against the railing at the bow of the ship. He watched the curving knife edge of the prow slash methodically into the marching procession of whitecaps, the water curling away to either side of the bow, half as high as the deck, in black sheets. The lifting crash of the bow against the waves set the entire ship to shuddering under the sharp concussive shocks. He stayed there watching, wondering what they were deciding below, feeling that he had made a fool of himself with his outbursts.

He turned and clambered back to Charlie's tank, hoping that at least if they didn't have sense enough to put a stop to the Vietnamese foolishness, they would have brains enough to clear out of the strait as fast as possible.

CHAPTER SIX

When Keilty returned to the wardroom an hour later, he found himself stopped at the hatch by a marine guard with a Sten gun, fully cocked.

'Sorry, sir, but ye dinna go in there.'

Keilty looked the brawny Scotsman up and down, noticing the set and intelligent face, and decided against making a fuss.

'Do me a favor,' he said. 'Get Admiral Rawingson out here. He'll get me a pass or whatever the devil I need.'

The marine hesitated a moment, then turned and spoke briefly into the intercom. The hatch opened seconds later.

'There you are,' Rawingson growled. 'Wondered where you got to.' He put a hand on Keilty's shoulder and pulled him in, saying to the guard, 'It's all right, Corporal, we need him in here.'

As Keilty entered, he noticed that now, not only was the cooling system prevailing against the pre-monsoon heat, but cooler heads prevailed also. The men were grouped around a large map tacked on the display board at the end of the room. There was no more angry discussion, nor were insults or imprecations being tossed back and forth. Instead, they were listening closely to the American Secretary of Defense as he carefully went through the various alternatives. Keilty moved halfway into the room and perched on a table. He pulled a cigarette from the pack in his shirt pocket and thumbed an old, worn Zippo to light it, then settled down to listen. Rawingson sat down on the bench below him and bummed a cigarette, then turned his attention also to the map.

The map was a larger version of the one Rawingson had shown him two days before. Over it, a sheet of acetate was taped, with grease-pencil markings indicating, first of all, the location of the bomb, then the currents in the strait and the surrounding area.

The *Bradley*'s meteorological officer had drawn in red the wind currents in the vicinity. A black area shaped like a many-pointed star was located in the Celebes marking the spawning grounds of the summer monsoon. Black arrows also extended northwestward across the Indonesian islands and into the Bay of Bengal to the west of Burma. A series of numbers that Keilty could not read from where he sat probably indicated expected times of arrival along the monsoon path.

Directly north, over southern China and North Vietnam and extending west to Thailand, the limits of a high-pressure area were drawn in green. This presumably was forcing the monsoon to approach more slowly than usual.

'It is our feeling,' the American Secretary of Defense was saying, 'that they have been planning this attack which they call "Operation Malacca" for quite some time now. They have been extremely fortunate that the weather has furnished such a large high-pressure front.' He indicated the area from the China Sea to Thailand, 'It is producing fair and very dry weather in the North and very shortly will turn the South into a sea of mud and rain. This will aid their movements down the Peninsula, while at the same time it will hamper Allied forces in Malaya if we are forced to evacuate from Kuala Lumpur and Singapore.

'The weather will certainly not hamper the insurgents in crossing the strait to Malaya, Singapore, and Borneo. For one thing, we will have lost almost our total straits fleet, so they will have no trouble from that quarter.

'By crossing,' he continued, 'in small craft under the cover of wind and low rain clouds, our bombing will be reduced to almost complete uselessness. Personally, I don't think they will make any trouble south into India. Since the Red Chinese lost their influence in Vietnam, the Soviets have been counting on India to contain China from that direction.'

'What happens,' Keilty asked suddenly, 'if the Indonesian Communist Party joins with the Malaysian Communists in a drive across Sumatra as well as up the Malay Peninsula? They just might figure it is time to act again, this time backed by the Vietnamese.'

The Secretary gave him a long, sad look. 'Your point is well taken, Dr. Keilty. It is just one more of the many possible alternatives to consider.' He was speaking now to the representative of the Indonesian army who shifted uncomfortably.

'You can depend on the fact that the Soviet Union is weighing all possibilities. Consider this. If Malaya falls to the Communists, then the line up in Indo-China will be complete. Thailand remains squeezed but possibly neutral only as long as it takes the Burmese Communists to upset their government and . . . they are not far from that point now. Then Thailand loses any remaining independence she would have. Cambodia and Laos fall into line without a whimper. With friendly Communist governments throughout the Peninsula, Singapore and its naval base falls right into the Soviet's lap as its main base in the South China Sea . . . controlling the approaches to the Straits from either direction and completing the encirclement of China. China is hemmed in and we are pushed back onto Australia and New Zealand. How long can Indonesia remain independent with insurgents and arms pouring across the Straits? How long can the Philippines remain independent if the South China Sea is a Russian lake?

'Strategic long-range interests make it imperative that the installation be destroyed or neutralized at the very least.' He shifted in his chair and relit his pipe. 'Recognize that the Soviets take no chances here. It all falls on the Vietnamese who recognize that their stake is very, very high . . . and they have always shown themselves willing to gamble against the odds.'

'Way too many alternatives, aren't there?' Keilty commented.

'Way too many,' the Secretary of Defense agreed dryly.

An Indonesian Admiral spoke up, his soft accent harshened by anger. 'What do we wait for? We have no choice but to act now.' He turned to the *Bradley*'s captain. 'If your weather reports are correct, we can no longer delay. To do so will be to see Singapore blanketed by radioactive water.'

'Admiral Okhato is correct, gentlemen,' an Australian officer said quietly. 'Do you want to see another Fall of Singapore like in forty-two. I don't, I was there. If we have to evacuate the bases at the same time everyone in the city is trying to get across the river, our chaps will die of radioactive poisoning. There's three million people in that city, two bridges to the mainland, and the causeway. If the monsoon strikes the day or so following the detonation, the insurgents could occupy a clean city and chase us so far back into the hills it will be the Japanese war all over again.'

There was a growl of agreement from the others. After several minutes of arguing, during which the American secretary remained aloof, he banged on the glass top of the chart table with a coffee cup. There was immediate silence.

'I propose,' he said simply, 'that the station be captured and the bombs be disarmed.'

A chorus of seconds greeted his proposal, and minutes later, they were again grouped around the maps, planning the best use of the *Bradley*, the two MTBs and the four companies of marines, two Australian/New Zealand combined units and one each Malaysian and Indonesian.

Two hours later, Keilty went below to the crew's mess, where Charlie had been installed, and found him swapping dirty jokes with the third-watch cook.

'Hey, you clown,' he roared. 'Cut that out, I got enough trouble with him as it is, without you putting more ideas into his head.'

The cook, who had not heard him come in, jumped in surprise, then swung around to see a blond giant with a bright red face bearing down on him. The door to the pantry was open and he made it in record time to the laughter of the other mess workers. Mumbling to himself, Keilty fussed around the tank, checking the water-temperature gauge and recirculating pump to Charlie's soft chuckles.

'For crying out loud,' Keilty said angrily. 'Where in hell did you pick up that kind of language?'

'Damned bluenose,' Charlie shot back, then laughed again, the sound coming out in static, as the transphonemator could not transliterate it.

'Look here, those numbskulls have finally decided to raid the station after all.'

'Do tell,' Charlie muttered. 'Another triumph of common sense.'

'Huh? Well, yeah, I guess you could call it that,' Keilty said with a glance at the dolphin that could only be described as fishy. He was beginning to wonder about Charlie. It was turning out that the dolphin was even sharper intellectually than he had thought. This whole fiasco was becoming a real eyeopener.

Keilty dragged up a chair, and with his feet on the seat, settled himself on the back so that he could look down into the tank. The dolphin was lying relaxed in the water. Charlie had pushed the mike extension around so that he could shift his position without banging into it. Keilty placed his mike in the clip on the edge of the tank and hunched forward comfortably to speak into it.

'So they decided to capture the station and get the bomb,' Charlie reiterated. 'How?'

'Well, as for the station, a straightforward attack is about the only way. Those pictures you brought back show only one narrow ladder, and the deck about sixty feet above the surface.

So the ladder will be the hardest part. You didn't see any other ladders, did you?' he asked sharply.

'Nope.'

'Well that's that, then. The ladder is the only way up.' Keilty paused. 'The stairs will be too well guarded.

'The seas are getting up a bit, and it's beginning to rain pretty hard out there. They tell me it will last about three hours, then quit. After that, the seas should keep rising. So they can depend on that for some cover.'

'That doesn't sound so difficult. I don't know much about this kind of nonsense,' Charlie said, 'but there shouldn't be too much trouble, should there?'

'Yep.' Keilty decided the back of the chair wasn't very comfortable and shifted down to the seat. 'There's a report that a Vietnamese destroyer – a ship like this one – is heading for the station. That could cause all sorts of trouble. They want to keep the carnage and bloodshed down as much as possible because of quote, world opinion, unquote, and if that destroyer shows up and starts shooting, there's going to be a mess.'

'Why not do it all and get it over with before the destroyer shows up?' Charlie asked.

'Because what's to prevent the destroyer from standing off and lobbing a few shells in to destroy the station – and the evidence!' He stressed the last.

'Oh.'

'So they need some way to knock off the destroyer, without sinking it if possible, and make it turn back.'

'So where's the problem? Get some help.'

'I figured you'd say that, 'cause that's what I asked.'

'And ...'

'And they told me. There's nothing that could do the job that could intercept the Vietnamese destroyer before it's too late. Everyone is either down the strait or back in Singapore, so they don't cause too much of a ruckus down here. Aircraft are out too,' he said to forestall Charlie's next question, 'because of the weather. There's only about two thousand feet visibility out there, even when it's not raining under these clouds. And radar isn't accurate enough for this job.'

Charlie digested all of this for a minute, then said: 'So what do they want us to do?'

Keilty stood up and rubbed the back of his neck, wondering how to put this next to the dolphin. He paced a moment, aware that the dolphin's great, clear eyes were on him, then abruptly sank back down into the chair.

'It's like this,' he began. 'They have what they call a limpet mine. You set a timer, clamp it to a ship with its built-in magnet, and when the timer runs out, the mine explodes and blows a hole in the ship. The timer lets the guy who planted it get away, or lets the ship get out to sea so that it sinks beyond the possibility of salvage.'

'And with this wonderful device . . .' Charlie spoke his unfinished sentence in an exceedingly dry voice.

'Now cut that out,' Keilty snapped, irritated.

'They want us – you – to plant this bomb, plant it just so, so that it will blow a God-damned big hole in the ship and force them to turn back.'

'They do, do they?' Charlie glared at him, then dropped his head below the water line.

'Hey, come on out of there,' Keilty yelled, and slapped the water. When nothing happened, he sat grimly back to wait.

Exactly two minutes later, Charlie stuck his head out of the water again. He glared at Keilty for a long moment.

'Do I have to wear that blasted pack again?'

'No. I can make up a sling for you to carry the mine beneath your chest. It only weighs ten pounds or so, and isn't very big.'

Charlie considered again. 'So what do I have to do?'

Keilty took a deep breath. It looked as if the dolphin would help after all. Suddenly it occurred to him. Why was he getting so worked up about this phase of the operation? They had done what they had been asked: verified the presence of the bomb. The rest of it was up to that pack of short-sighted idiots still arguing in the wardroom. He shrugged mentally. Somebody had to do it, and it looked as if they were elected. A germ of an idea occurred to him. His face took on a strangely piratical appearance, his heavy blond brows drawing inward and down. He ran a blunt hand through the straw-colored mop of hair and stood thinking a moment.

'Hey. I said, what do I have to do?' Charlie's demand snapped his train of thought. He grinned at the dolphin.

'My friend, we are going to make a killing. All you gotta do is take the mine. The first MTB – on which I will also be – will take you out and drop you in the path of the destroyer. You hang around until it comes up. It should only be doing fifteen knots or so, and you won't have any trouble in catching it as it goes by. When you do, plant the mine close to the bottom of the keel, just back of the bow where it begins to flatten out. Figure it's about twenty feet back from the front. The mine has a magnet, so it will stick. As soon as it makes contact with the hull, the mine will go off in exactly fifteen minutes. So you get out of there as fast as possible. Swim back the way you came, and you should be able to spot the second MTB with your sonar. They will take you back to the *Bradley*. Then join us as reinforcements.

'Our MTB will have to drop you, then beat it for the station. The second MTB will have to hang back a couple of miles so that the destroyer doesn't spot them on radar. You won't have any trouble finding them with your sonar, will you?' Keilty asked anxiously. 'Or the destroyer either?'

'Noooo, I wouldn't think so,' Charlie answered dryly. He was about to add something about the quality of the human underwater gear, then thought better of it.

'All right, if that's all there is to it, you can tell them they've got a minelayer.' Charlie hesitated. 'That's a joke, son.'

'Yeah, I know,' Keilty said with a straight face, and stood up. 'Look now, get some rest. I'll go back and tell those clowns you're willing and maybe dicker with them.' He patted Charlie's rough gray head and went out, after warning the mess crew to let the dolphin rest.

This time the marine guard saluted and opened the hatch quickly.

'Thanks,' Keilty said, and stepped in. The loud buzz of conversation died down as he made his way between the tables to the map. When he reached it, he turned his back to the bulkhead and grinned at the expectant faces.

'Gentlemen, he agrees.'

Several heads nodded at this wise choice, except Rawingson's. Keilty noticed he was staring at him with a slightly quizzical look.

He held up a hand, grinning wolfishly. 'Our fee will be one hundred and fifty thousand U.S. dollars. A letter of commitment, signed by you . . .' He turned to the American Secretary of State, who looked rather thunderstruck. '. . . and witnessed by the rest, will do for now.'

Angry voices began shouting and arguing. 'And,' he finished with a roar to override the noise, 'it will be payable on demand and of course subject to G and A fees and overhead.'

It took forty-five minutes of bland indifference to the shouting, but eventually he pocketed the letter of commitment.

They spent a sickening ten minutes getting Charlie's tank transferred from the rolling and pitching *Bradley* to the MTB, bobbing and dancing beneath the black wall of steel that was the destroyer. Keilty could imagine the sweating face and strained muscles of the helmsman as he fought the wheel to keep the relatively tiny craft from being crushed by the larger destroyer. From the sound of the engines, both Rolls Royce gas turbines must have been turning over at maximum power.

Keilty had supervised the rigging of the transfer line himself and had inflated the oil-filled sacs that would cushion Charlie in place of water. The dolphin had said nothing the entire time, although Keilty had left the transphonemator in place and working so that he could soothe the highly nervous dolphin. He had noted with concern that the tension had drawn strong lines around Charlie's beak and eyes and lines along his body that shifted constantly with his muscle action.

Deep black clouds filled the sky from horizon to horizon and pressed down closely on the three frail craft in the center of a dark, empty universe. The barometer needle had been dropping slowly all day, and strangely enough, there had been no wind. Only a leaden silence broken by the muted roar of engines and the quiet slap of feet. Talk in the oppressive atmosphere was limited to desultory conversation and occasional commands.

The destroyer's floodlights had been turned on at the bow and along the starboard side to provide light for the MTB crews. Their own running lights added to the harsh glare that surrounded the three ships. Looking down from the railing to the deck of the frantically bobbing MTB, Keilty could see angry waves with foamy crests lashing upwards like solid metal hulks before sliding brokenly back into oily troughs. Once overboard in that, he thought, if you weren't crushed against one side or another, the giant twin screws of the destroyer, or the smaller, sharper ones of the MTBs would make mincemeat out of you. Providing you escaped that fate, you would be lost forever in the eight-foot seas.

The lights from the ships, a bright pool in the ocean of darkness, created a scene strongly reminiscent of an Ingmar Bergman movie. The whites were crystalline and harsh and the blacks were pools of jet, with no shade of gray or color in between. Except for the fluidity of movement, the slow-motion rise and fall of the man-made ships, and the wild insanity of the sea, the scene could have been that of a lunar rock formation at sunset. He wished he had a camera to record the drama so he could later compare the scene with photos taken by various Apollo Lunar Expeditions. He was sure that he would find the same breathless prescience of danger that almost screamed from the two-dimensional recordings of man's attack on what was essentially alien territory.

Turning away from the rail, he tried to shake off his sinister and superstitious dread. He said a few words to Charlie, who did not reply, and he noted the clear whites that showed completely around his pupils. Like a frightened horse, he thought ... or a man.

He stroked the dolphin's head and was about to say something else, when the iron voice of the PA system boomed at him.

'Are you set down there, Dr. Keilty?'

He waved back at the bridge and caught snatches of muffled conversation with the MTB carrying over the loudspeakers.

'Prepare to transfer tank. Cargo officer, at your discretion.' The flat, metallic voice died quickly with no trace of answering echo. Keilty shivered again. Charlie must have caught his mood, because he looked up at Keilty and dropped one eyelid in a close approximation of a wink.

Feeling slightly relieved, Keilty swung himself up onto the tank so that he was astride one of the oil cushions beneath the middle tackle guy.

The cargo officer came over at a run. 'Dr. Keilty, you can't go over on that.' The fear in his voice was obvious to all.

Trying to keep his voice calm, Keilty replied, 'Why not? You guys said it was safe.' It didn't come off, and his voice was harsh with suppressed fear.

'Of course it's safe. But if something should go ...'

'God damn it. If it's safe, nothing will go wrong. You think I'm going to let him ride across if the whole lousy system's going to fall apart?'

The officer, his face screwed up with doubt, hesitated, then turned on his heel and ran back to the bosun's chair lying on the deck next to the winch. He was back quickly with a wide safety strap.

'Put this around your waist and secure it to the tackle lock. If something goes wrong, it's got a quick-release buckle. Lift up on the right side.' He hesitated again and looked up at Keilty as he took the belt. 'Good luck, sir,' he said quietly, and went back to the winch.

Keilty finished buckling up the belt and glanced up at the bridge. A line of faces pressed against the window, but the angle and light made it impossible to make out features. He rapped Charlie on the back and waved a hand at the cargo officer.

The tank jerked, then swung crazily for a moment until the winches took up the slack in the guide ropes.

'Here we go, ugly,' he muttered through clenched teeth.

'Looked in a mirror lately?' was Charlie's strained reply.

The tank lifted smoothly for a moment, then dropped sickeningly over the rail and began the long slide down to the jouncing deck below. Behind, Keilty could see the destroyer out of the corner of his eye as the deck dropped below them. He jerked his head around in time to see the MTB ride up a crest.

'Christ,' he roared. 'Hang on . . .'

The cable above his head whipsawed sharply and the tank sprang upwards, then violently down as the destroyer rode up again. The winch screamed behind him at the overload, smoke pouring from the motor housing as the cable sawed into the reel.

Then, as suddenly as it had begun, the tank was level again and seconds later thumped onto the deck, where it was securely bolted down. Keilty painfully pried his fingers loose from the guy wire and turned on his stomach and slid down stiffly.

'How the hell did I ever get mixed up with you?' Charlie asked wearily.

Five minutes later, the two MTBs were beating their way southeast through steadily worsening seas.

CHAPTER SEVEN

Keilty crouched on the lee side of the MTB's cabin, watching through the aft hatch the radio operator with his head cocked to one side and earphones held with both hands to his ears. The man's face tightened for a moment, then he reached for his pencil and began scribbling out the message. Keilty looked at the huge Maori beside him in the camouflage greens of the Royal New Zealand Marines with the pips of a lieutenant. When the radio operator nodded vigorously at them, the Maori smiled broadly and went below to chivvy up his troops. Keilty remained where he was, crouching into the open hatchway to escape the cold, blowing spray that was spuming back from the bow. He, like Charlie, was wondering how he had ever gotten himself involved in this mess.

Ten miles to the southeast, the Vietnamese destroyer was coming fast. The sea conditions, which were worsening steadily, had hidden them from the destroyer's surface radar when they had dropped Charlie minutes earlier, and they were now roaring northwest in the direction of the research station. Charlie, with the limpet bomb, was waiting for the destroyer. If everything went off according to plan, the mine would explode in about twenty minutes and the destroyer would be damaged severely enough to have to turn back in these heavy seas. Keilty had spent twenty minutes on the run south explaining to Charlie just how and where to plant the bomb.

The message that had just come in was from the *Bradley*. Two Indonesian destroyers were rushing up from Sumatra and an Australian mine layer from Singapore was on its way to supplement the *Bradley*, but wouldn't arrive for at least eight hours or better. The two MTBs were detailed to go in immediately Charlie was recovered and word was received that the Vietnamese destroyer was out of action. They would land their component of marines under covering fire if necessary. The station must be secured as fast as possible to prevent the crew on board destroying the bomb and the evidence that it had been prepared for this special operation.

Keilty looked at his watch in the dim glow from the interior of the small bridge. Just about five minutes to go. He hoped that the second MTB had not missed Charlie in the stormy seas. Peter Owterry, the Maori lieutenant, slid in next to him, grinning from ear to ear.

'All set on this end. It promises to be a bloody good show . . .'

Keilty raised his hand. 'Quiet a second.' And indicated the radio operator scribbling on his pad again.

He tore off the sheet and handed it to the boat's commander, who swung round, and grinning from ear to ear, said, 'Looks as if your dolphin made it, Dr. Keilty. He's been picked up, and without the mine.'

Suddenly, the storm-shrouded horizon was lit by a brilliant flash, revealing heavy clouds banked tier on tier. As if waiting for the signal of the explosion, sheets of lightning ripped the sky, and were followed by heavy rolls of thunder; rain poured down on the small boat, causing a steady drumming. Before Keilty could pull his slicker tight around him, he was soaked clear to the skin by the heavy drops. The rain cut effective visibility to next to nothing.

Owterry, staring up into the driving rain, laughed. 'This rain is certainly going to be a help. It seems that the elements are conspiring with us instead of against us for a change. The rain will hide us from lookouts and the waves from surface radar.'

The radioman interrupted again to announce that the flash had been the explosion of the Vietnamese destroyer. The *Bradley*'s radar showed she was steaming at about four knots for the nearest point of land, which was the extreme southern tip of Sumatra.

Keilty hung on to the bridge stanchion as the deck whipped beneath his feet. The MTB, taking the full brunt of the pounding waves, leapt from wave to wave in the heavy seas. The rain fell harder and was thrashed by the wind into the flying spray until it seemed to be a solid sheet of water.

The two boats hammered on northward skirting the larger of the islands until shortly before dawn, when the commander throttled down. Keilty went down into the cramped cabin where he could watch the radar building a picture of the research station. The short-range sweep showed the *Bradley* some ten miles west, steaming on at close to thirty-five knots. The British commander swore softly to himself when he heard the *Bradley*'s speed.

'She was built during the latter part of the war,' he said to Keilty in his soft west-country accent. 'She must be taking a terrible pounding in these seas.' Then he brightened, 'I'll bet all those high muckety-mucks aboard are wishing they could die.'

Keilty agreed whole-heartedly with the picture.

The MTB came round the tower at almost full power in a heeling, skidding turn that would have done credit to an outboard. Her sister ship broke off to rendezvous with the *Bradley*.

Keilty wondered how Charlie was taking all this. His conscience had been bothering him since Charlie had gone overboard. Events had moved too fast for the dolphin to keep up with them. He had been confused and nervous, and if Keilty had not known better, he would have thought the dolphin was scared silly. But the animal's nervous condition *was* close to actual human fear. He had almost huddled in his tank aboard the tossing craft, his flippers and tail making fluttering motions against the side of the tank, his eyes rolling back until the whites showed against his almost black skin. Keilty had done his best to calm him, stroking his flanks, moistening him with a large sponge and promising a long, quiet airplane ride when this was all over.

Keilty knew that the dolphin was aware that this mission was much more dangerous than the other. He would be completely detached from Keilty and would not even see him when it was over. He would be depending on others to look after him and pick him up. In addition, the storm had frightened him. He had never been involved in a surface storm before, and the lashing waves and the tossing motion of the boat were rapidly giving him a classic case of seasickness. But then, when it came time to put him over the side, these symptoms disappeared and the dolphin shot over the side and sounded deeply. Keilty only hoped he had not been frightened so badly that he would revert to his native state.

Owterry plopped down beside him and shrugged out of his slicker. 'Have to clear the decks for action,' he said cheerfully. 'Can't move at all in that blasted thing. Besides, I couldn't get any wetter.'

He peered over the side at the thrashing waves and then to where the bulk of the station could be seen dimly outlined against the black sky. 'Looks like we may have to go in under fire. The *Bradley*'s not in position yet and she couldn't fire from where she is without hitting us.'

'Hell of a fine fix to be in on a night like this,' Keilty muttered. He shrugged his shoulders against the pelting rain that was seeping beneath his collar and down his neck. The deck boards had a nasty habit of dropping away suddenly and then smacking hard against him as the boat slammed sharply upwards. The MTB tightened the circled approach until she was less than a hundred yards away from the tower. Owterry climbed unsteadily to his feet for a better look.

'Damned station's awfully quiet. . .' As if waiting for just this cue, the Vietnamese opened up with a withering blast of light-arms fire. Keilty pressed himself into the deck to escape the hail of lead that stitched into the hull with amazing accuracy. Owterry dropped half on top of him, squirmed into the open hatchway, and then reached a huge hand up and around Keilty and dragged him in. He caught a glimpse of the second MTB returning off their stern.

'Captain,' he shouted against the screaming of the wind and engines, 'can you run us in under the deck of the tower?'

Keilty looked at him slowly. It would be suicide to get in under the deck in these seas. One heavy wave could crush them against a supporting column, or even the underside of the deck. The commander obviously thought so too, but Owterry rushed on before he could interrupt.

'Get in under the overhang of the deck and around to the far side of that ladder. MTB two-oh-three can stand off and sweep the decks with machine-gun fire until the *Bradley* gets here. By that time, we should be aboard.' He paused to take a quick look at the tower, illuminated now by heavy flashes of lightning and by the quick, small flashes of the fire fight. The accuracy of the station gunners' aim had fallen off drastically in the heavy seas. As Keilty watched, the station was hidden from view by a large wave until only the upper works of the tower showed. As they crested the station was in full view, and then lost again.

'Once we get in and onto the ladder, you put out quickly and keep them busy around the top of the ladder so they can't get to us,' Owterry finished.

It took Owterry only a few minutes to convince the boat's commander that, under the circumstances, it was the only way to secure the research station and the bomb.

Signals were made to MTB 203 advising her of the plan and then to the *Bradley*. With the commander at the wheel and the twin Rolls turbines screaming to full rpm, the boat went in on a straight course from a point two hundred yards from the ladder. The MTB sliced through the heaving seas at forty-five knots, bouncing like a surfboard, then straightened out and beat her way through the twenty-foot waves. Water boiled around her stern from the creaming bow wave, sweeping half as high as the slanted mast. Keilty, crouching in the bow with the initial ten-man landing party, hung on for dear life. He hung back slightly, trying to stay out of Owterry's view. The New Zealander was busy trying to gauge the distance and the effect of the shells and bullets that were beginning to converge on 202.

Keilty watched the big Maori at work, marveling at the calmness of his Oxfordian voice deeply resounding above the racket of the storm. Earlier, one of the marines had proudly told him that Owterry was educated in England at St. James, had been New Zealand boxing champion, and had almost taken the Commonwealth boxing crown until the war interrupted. Owterry himself had told him that he had fought from Burma down the Malay Peninsula in 1944–45, and then back up against the Communists in 1947–50.

'You're lucky we're in the strait and not on the mainland,' Owterry had grinned. 'This is relatively clean. Malaya has jungles like nowhere else on earth.'

Keilty had noticed the leech scars on his hands, wrists, and ankles, and mentioned them.

'A doctor once told me that the scars on my ankles form a ring of scar tissue nearly an inch deep,' he had replied. After that, Keilty was prepared to believe anything about Southeast Asian jungles.

The distance was now less than a hundred yards. A flurry of light 1.5-inch shells splashed and exploded dead ahead of them. The concussion and the water they kicked up almost washed Keilty over the side. The commander kept the boat steady on its course. Keilty watched the tower loom ahead of them, seeming to grow larger with infinite slowness. A second salvo hit closer, bracketing the boat and lifting the bow high in the air. For a moment it hung suspended.

Keilty had time to notice that the rain, which had become almost horizontal in the wind, was no longer pelting him for a brief second as the hull came between him and the watery horizon. Then the MTB slapped down hard, jarring every bone in his body. He tasted blood in his mouth where a tooth was broken. His back was on fire where the FN carbine on its loose sling had crashed down. Dazedly he noticed that the boat was skidding into a hard starboard turn as the engines cut out and then screamed up as the propellers reversed and the boat slid under the overhang, port quarter first.

The commander idled the engines down enough to maintain steerageway and turned her towards the single narrow ladder, outlined dimly by the hooded beam of the boat's searchlight. They drew alongside the ladder and were held fast by two ratings as they piled over the side into two rubber life rafts. Keilty was the last over. He ignored Owterry's shout, and watching the bobbing raft, jumped and landed half across the stern and was hauled into the bottom of the raft.

'Where the hell do you think you're going?' Owterry stormed at him from the other raft.

'Where the hell do you think?' Keilty shouted back. 'Stop yelling and let's get going. I've got a vested interest in this operation.'

Owterry waved the MTB away. It idled away from them and then slipped into full power and shot from beneath the deck, its two quad .50s blazing away at the station decking. Keilty watched it roar away, swinging in a wide circle to allow the gunners to track their target, and then he lost it in the rain and fog.

The noise of the fighting came to them in a mishmash of hollow sound, reflected from beneath the steel tower by the chopping seas. The rafts were made fast to the tower ladder and the combined units of New Zealand and Australian marines swarmed up first, followed by the Indonesian unit. They had shed their packs on the MTB and wore only shirts and shorts, with their weapons slung over their shoulders within easy reach to leave their hands free for the ladder. They went up professionally. Keilty was pushed back until he was last man on the ladder. Gunfire sounded above and a brief spray of bullets swept past him. A body came hurtling down; which side, he was unable to tell.

Then he was being yanked over the top and pushed down behind a hastily constructed barrier of empty oil drums. Owterry was waving four men around the far edge of the barrier in a flanking movement to the drilling rig. Snipers in the rig took two of the men before they had taken five steps. Cursing horribly, his eyes white-rimmed in the flashing lightning, Owterry landed beside him, directing a barrage of fire to the rigging. Keilty unslung his carbine, worked the slide to make sure it wasn't jammed, and aimed at a figure crouching behind a web of bracing halfway up the tower. He fired three shots and missed. Rain water sluiced down the barrel and spattered into his eyes. He shook his head and rubbed his eyes clear, ignoring the stinging, then turned his attention back to the sniper. He slid the catch to full automatic and opened up. The figure straightened, took a quick step backwards, arched its back, and sailed off into space. He landed with a sodden thump on the steel deck plates. Grinning savagely, Keilty jammed another magazine home.

Across the deck near the main shaft of the tower, were a series of low corrugated-iron sheds. As Keilty glanced towards them seeking another target, the door in the nearest one was flung open and four men poured out. They dove for positions around the shaft, setting up a machine gun. The entire movement was performed so quickly that it took the marines off guard. The machine gun opened up fast. Keilty ducked back around the oil drums just in time. A sharp clang, and a steel sliver was nicked from the drum where his head had been. The machine gun traversed the row of drums and was followed by rifle fire, while the gunners turned their attention to the two men who had reached the rig. They were all now effectively pinned down. Keilty ducked back deeper into the safety of the oil drums. Owterry yelled something that was lost in the rattle of the machine gun and the series of clangs from the drums.

The man next to Keilty struggled into a sitting position while he fumbled in his shirt. Then, going to his knees, he straightened up and started to hurl a hand grenade. Two fifty-caliber slugs stitched across his chest and he fell back, dropping the live grenade into Keilty's lap. Keilty was so surprised that he stared stupidly for a moment, then straightened convulsively and kicked out with his foot, pitching the grenade over the side of the deck where it exploded. Owterry rolled his eyes to heaven – whether in thankfulness or supplication, Keilty could not tell. Then the machine gun was back.

Keilty could now see the two flankers clearly. And they were clearly pinned down. They had depended on the main party to furnish them with covering fire while they flanked and came up on the main body of the defenders holding the deck. Now that the main party was pinned down, they were exposed to a flanking movement themselves and this was precisely what was happening to them. From their left, three Vietnamese soldiers were crawling towards the party, using the cover furnished by equipment and machinery. The flankers were kept pinned by the machine gun and could not effectively cover themselves.

Keilty pulled the remaining two grenades from the shirt of the dead marine. The pictures that Charlie had gotten from the sea had shown a small ledge running the circumference of the top of the main deck. It was only about five feet below the level of the deck, but it had looked wide enough to walk on.

Ignoring Owterry, he crawled back to the ladder, careful to keep the drums between himself and the machine gun. One of the snipers in the rig saw him and began firing. The bullets slammed and ricocheted viciously around him. With one sliding leap, Keilty grabbed the edge of the ladder and all but vaulted over. His foot caught the rung and he yanked his head down below the deck.

The ledge was there, but it was not really a ledge, more of a catwalk with ladderlike rungs. He crouched down and slung his rifle with one hand, being careful to keep one hand on the ladder. The wind had picked up now and was blowing close to thirty knots. The rain pelted down in huge, swollen drops that all but blinded him. He worked the hand grenades into his pockets and began inching his way along, carefully placing one foot on the rung ahead, hanging on to the slippery edge of the decking. The wind tore at him, pulling at his sodden shirt and Levis. In spite of the waterproofing he had applied earlier in the day, his leather boots were soaked through with the heavy monsoon rains.

After what seemed an eternity, he stopped and raised his head carefully above the decking. He could see the dim outline of the barrels and to his right, still some fifty feet away and hidden by the machinery, the flashes of the machine gun.

The wind was now so loud in his ears that nothing else seemed real. The flashes of the guns were soundless in the immensity of roaring wind and water. He lowered his head and started forward again. Once he slipped and caught himself only by his fingers from falling into the water seventy feet below. He managed to hook a leg around a rung and rested for a moment. Then he was moving ahead again. He never knew how long it actually took him, but it seemed forever.

At the end of another hundred feet, he stopped and raised his head for a careful look. Almost in front of him and some fifty feet away, crouched the gunner and the man feeding the belt. On the other side, two riflemen with automatic weapons were firing carefully and accurately over the top of the rigging machinery.

Keilty levered himself up into a half crouch, one leg hooked around a support rod. He fumbled with a grenade which resisted his efforts to pull it from his wet pocket. He cursed the tight Levis he was wearing. Keilty had made a turn coming around the edge of the decking, so that he was now taking the full force of the wind against his right side. The wind was becoming fitful now, rising from its steady thirty knots until it was almost a full gale, then dropping suddenly with no warning. Every time it rose, Keilty had to stop and hang on to keep from being blown off the tower.

Finally, in desperation he straightened his legs, and half bending from the waist to keep his head below the level of the deck as much as possible, Keilty yanked the hand grenade free. He shoved the narrow end with the lever into his mouth. The weight of the steel ground down on his broken tooth, making him gasp in pain. He almost lost the grenade, but managed to hang on, fighting the waves of nausea that threatened to make him vomit. He transferred it to the other hand and worked the other grenade loose in his pocket. For a second, he caught a brief glimpse of a raft in the flickering lightning, full of men, pulling to the ladder as the wind screamed around them.

The machine gun was now concentrating its fire on the barrels and the top of the gangway. The flashes from the muzzle were almost a steady stream of fire. Keilty straightened as much as he could, aware that he was silhouetted against the lightning-filled sky. With his teeth, he twisted loose the pin on the grenade in his left hand, then transferred it carefully to his right hand, careful to keep the lever down tightly. He tried to judge the wind, waiting for a lull, then threw with an overhand swing and missed. The grenade landed short and well to the left of the machine gun, bounced once, and exploded harmlessly.

Keilty straightened again, peering over the edge of the decking. Rifle slugs whined past his ears as he pulled the pin on the second grenade. The men ahead were frantically swinging the machine gun around as he threw the grenade with all his strength and ducked. The grenade hit and skidded across the deck, bouncing directly towards the spitting rifles, and exploded under the tripod of the machine gun. Pieces of steel whined away into the night.

Keilty edged his head up. Lightning showed the rip pipe

racks directly above the gunners to be a shambles. The twisted barrel of the machine gun lay against the dented side of the cabin. The grenade had exploded between the rig and the cabin, funneling the exploding shrapnel both ways, mowing down the four men like paper cutouts. They lay strewn at odd angles on the deck.

Owterry and his men rushed the cabin from the cover of the barrels, clearing the last of the defenders from the deck and rigging on the way.

Keilty climbed stiffly over the edge of the deck and stood up slowly. He could see the raft-load of marines begin to appear around the top of the ladder, slowly at first, then more quickly as they met with no resistance. They paid no attention to him standing in the shadows, his carbine still slung, but disappeared below after Owterry.

There were only a few white lights still burning in the rigging, and the red warning light over the cabin's wrecked door. Somehow it had escaped the bullets and exploding shrapnel.

Keilty followed below after the last squad. He caught up with them at the beginning of a corridor that led into the center of the station. The interior was laid out in a triangular fashion some two hundred feet across at the base and three levels deep. The corridor down which they were now moving cautiously, led to the sleeping quarters and mess hall. Bare, unfrosted bulbs were glowing dimly from the ceiling and the steel walls, painted a deep gray, reflected little of the meager light. The marines moved slowly down the corridor, five to each side. They stopped once to check what appeared to be an empty office, its door half opened. The corridor was the main passageway to the center of the station. At its end, it branched to the right and left. When the Royal Marines reached the junction, they cautiously poked a helmet around the corner. A flurry of shots rang out and the helmet spun down the left branch. A corporal armed with a tear-gas gun put the muzzle around the corner and fired two successive cylinders. Keilty, without a mask, beat a hasty retreat back to the deck.

The rain had steadied to an insistent needle drive that immediately drove him back into the shelter of the stairwell in the entrance to the cabin. The rain stabbed at his skin, ignoring the covering of his wet shirt and Levis. Through the rain, he caught sight of the dim silhouette of the *Bradley*, several cable lengths away. The destroyer was steaming slowly around the station to maintain steerageway in the heavy seas. As he watched, the destroyer focused two powerful searchlights on the tower, throwing details into sharp reliefs of black and white shadow that shifted constantly as the destroyer fought through the pounding waves.

More marines, slickered against the driving rain, were clambering over the side of the deck from a motor launch below. Another hatch was opened and they quickly disappeared below, leaving the deck suddenly deserted, except for three woebegone prisoners standing half drowned in the rain while their guard leaned negligently under the protecting overhang of a shed, his rifle circling slowly in their general direction.

Keilty stood listening to the wind screaming its high-pitched wail through the spiderwork of the tower, wishing mightily for a cigarette. He had just decided to go back down below decks to see what was happening, when five gas-masked marines came through the hatchway behind him, pushing a batch of prisoners, their hands clasped over their heads and their eyes streaming, and hurried them across the deck.

Owterry followed the prisoners. He caught sight of Keilty standing in the shelter of the cabin and came over.

'War's over,' he announced cheerfully. 'Thanks very much for your help, by the way,' Owterry added.

'Hooray,' Keilty muttered. 'I need a cigarette.'

Owterry hauled out a soaking packet of Players, glared at them in disgust, and threw them away. 'They're bringing up portable fans to blow out the tear gas,' he said. 'The place is full of it and somebody wrecked the air-conditioning system.'

He produced a spare gas mask and handed it to Keilty. 'Put this on and let's go take a look at the bomb. We got to it in plenty of time. Those idiots hadn't even attempted to get rid of it.'

They ducked into the thinning fog of tear gas that was rolling up the stairwell. Keilty noticed that someone had gotten the generators going again and the bulbs cast a considerably stronger light. They passed an office where several Vietnamese prisoners milled about sullenly, guarded by two marines with leveled weapons.

The tear gas had thinned out quite a bit and Keilty and Owterry removed their masks. He took a good look at the prisoners as they passed the office. Their clothes and hair were streaming with water which formed puddles on the incongruous green carpeting in the steel-bulkheaded room. They had the hard-bitten look of professional soldiers and they were alert and tense, in contrast to the three Keilty had seen on the deck. These were professionals, and the others had probably been scientists and technicians. The two guards appeared ready for trouble, with their carbines on full automatic and safetys off.

Owterry led him along a narrow catwalk, then down a vertical steel ladder into a featureless oval room. Keilty glanced back up the tube through which they had just climbed down, noting that it was a hydraulically operated telescoping tube.

In the center of the room, a steel case about the size of a pickup truck was placed. There were the usual meaningless dials that Keilty had expected, and when he walked up for a closer look, he noticed that they were labeled in Vietnamese. He looked around the room. Besides the case, which was on the raised platform where he stood, the room was completely bare. The room itself was lit by soft fluorescent lights. Keilty noted the incongruity of the General Electric trademark on the light fixtures and the Vietnamese letters on the bomb casing.

Suddenly, it occurred to him that *he* was standing in the same room with a five-megaton thermonuclear bomb. The bomb itself might be harmless without its trigger, but its radiations certainly were not. He moved quickly and grasped the arm of a marine leaning against the casing and yanked him away.

'Hey . . .'

'For the sake of your future offspring, friend. Have you checked this room for radiation?' he asked, turning to Owterry.

The New Zealander paled under his coppery skin. 'No . . .'

'Then I suggest we all get the devil out of here until those sorcerer's apprentices you people brought along get through in here.

'It's not going anywhere,' he added.

There was a hasty retreat up the ladder.

CHAPTER EIGHT

Keilty watched a Japanese freighter make its way slowly through the tangled knots of junks, freighters, pleasure craft, and warships anchored or moving in the roadstead below. Mariposa cluttered the slope for a short way below the hotel balcony on which he was standing and ended in a jumble of boulders and rocks leading to a sheer drop down to the narrow slice of land fronting the harbor below. He breathed deeply, inhaling the fragrance of the tropical sea breeze that mingled with the odors of fuel oil, rotting fish, and just plain Singapore.

To the east, barely visible around the jutting headland, was the electrified fence of the big naval base that climbed halfway up the slope before turning inland. Where the outcropping rock dipped inward, he had a clear view of the almost empty piers. While he watched, a flight of F-14's blasted across the harbor, hauled up, and disappeared around the headland. Moments later, a lone Canberra with British markings trundled across the harbor and slowly disappeared out to sea. Further out, past the harbor entrance, a giant Australian aircraft carrier was working around to the north to patrol along the New Guinea coast. Its escort of three destroyers and a guided-missile frigate flanked her on either side like ladies-in-waiting. A destroyer frisked ahead and he could just make out the foaming bow wave, curling back along the flanks of the leading frigate.

With a great deal of satisfaction he watched the busy scene in the harbor. Almost a week had passed since they had returned to Singapore and every day, signs of military activity had been decreasing. Rawingson had told him the day before that the U.S. Seventh Fleet was in the process of withdrawing from the straits area and standing down from the Red Alert imposed as soon as the scientists had confirmed the presence of a nuclear bomb in the research station.

Curiously enough, nothing had come of the entire affair, it seemed. The various governments involved had clamped a lid of tight secrecy on and so far it seemed to be holding except for some slight speculation in the world press. Nothing had been heard from the Vietnamese government, officially or unofficially, in response to the strong notes of protest passed secretly to them through the Kremlin. The Soviets had seemed to ignore the rebuke and had remained silent as well. Rawingson had reported with some glee that the Soviet probes into Sinkiang and along the Manchurian border which had been increasing in past weeks had stopped abruptly the day after the station was secured. He had taken this to mean that the Russians considered themselves checked.

Keilty straightened his broad, lanky frame and walked slowly back into the suite. He pulled off his shorts and went into the bathroom, plugged in his shaver and ran it over his long, muscular face, grinning at himself the entire time.

He was well pleased. A cablegram had come earlier from his Miami bank, notifying him that the one hundred and fifty thousand dollar fee had been promptly paid by the Department of Defense. He had picked up the phone happily and called the cable office and sent off a cable instructing the bank to pay off the long, long overdue bills. His last talk with the Secretary of Defense before he had left for Honolulu, a quiet, top-secret meeting, had resulted in a promise of new research contracts and the directorship of a newly established Dolphin Research Institute in the Florida Keys with a salary of $30,000 a year. He and Admiral Rawingson both had insisted it be put in writing immediately and he had his 'stated' copy in his bags. Rawingson was learning quickly too, he grinned.

Keilty took a quick shower and padded into the bedroom, toweling his sunburned body. He winced as the rough towel scraped across the plastic valve set into the skin between his spine and the right shoulder blade. As he dressed in a dark blue pair of slacks and a short-sleeved cotton shirt, he worried his damaged tooth with his tongue. It seemed to have reset itself properly, as the *Bradley*'s medical officer had told him it would. He knotted a thin blue tie, pulled on a madras jacket, and then stepped into a pair of loafers.

Keilty returned to the terrace and stood watching the magnificent scene superimposed on the placid waters of the harbor below, then left the room and hotel quickly.

Twenty minutes later, he was aboard the Australian cruiser *Vigilant*, sitting at a highly polished dark walnut table. An orderly placed a tall glass of scotch and water on the table and handed him an ornate menu.

Seated at the table with Keilty were Rawingson in neatly pressed whites, the gold braid gleaming inconspicuously; the captain of the *Vigilant*, Commander Whittlson; and a Michael J. Hallan, to whom Keilty had just been introduced. Hallan was a member of the CIA stationed in Indonesia. Next to Hallan was his opposite number in Australian Naval Intelligence in Djakarta, Ralston Hutchins. They were an oddly contrasting pair, Keilty thought; Hallan, short but spare, looking more like a small-town druggist than either a CIA operative or the sales representative for a farm equipment manufacturer, which was his cover. Hutchins, on the other hand, was very James Bondish – of medium height and rather a dark complexion, but with green eyes instead of blue, and Scandinavian features – with the exception of dark hair. His hair was brushed informally straight across and was dry looking. On meeting him, Keilty had immediately suspected that he was a good swimmer. As it turned out, Hutchins had taken two bronze medals and a gold one in the 1960 Olympics – the 100-meter freestyle, 100-meter dash and backstroke.

Also sitting at the table was a representative of the newly re-formed SEATO alliance – representing the U.S.,, United Kingdom, Australia, New Zealand, Thailand, Malaysia, Singapore, and the Philippines – Lieutenant General James Phillips, USAF.

Among so many uniforms, Keilty, Hutchins, and Hallan looked out of place, and as they took their seats at the table, they drew up chairs next to each other, as if for mutual support.

Vice-Admiral William Collins bustled into the cabin, nodding and muttering apologies for his lateness as he took his seat at the head of the table.

'Very sorry, gentlemen, unexpected delay. Hope you've been keeping our guests entertained, Commander,' he said jovially, turning to face the others, who nodded.

'Well in that case, shall we order lunch before we get down to cases.' He picked up his menu, then promptly put it down again, waving to the orderly hovering about the table with an order pad. 'My usual, Leslie.'

He swung round to Keilty, 'We meet again, Dr. Keilty. How do you find your stay in Singapore, sir? Rather delightful place, I have always thought, especially for a bachelor.' He laughed at the expression on Keilty's face.

Keilty let the smile come through. Peter Owterry, an old Singapore hand, had shown him the town before he shipped out two days before, and unknown to Keilty, had arranged with several establishments to keep Keilty well supplied with company. He had managed to get the latest one sent off less than two hours ago.

'Ha, I do see you find Singapore very congenial.' The admiral roared with laughter at his own cleverness.

The conversation degenerated into desultory small talk from there. The luncheon was served and Keilty found the Royal Australian Navy cooking – at least for admirals – to be excellent. The sole was baked to perfection and the seafood sauce had just the right amount of tang, suggesting a chef who knew the value of certain spices with seafood. Later, brandy and cigars were produced and the seven men lit up, the admiral explaining that this was an eccentricity of his, preferring a hearty midday dinner and a light supper at night.

'Well, gentlemen,' the admiral said, 'we all – with the exception of Dr. Keilty – know why we are here.' He beamed around the table.

'Leslie,' he shouted to the orderly. 'Take yourself ashore for the afternoon, never mind cleaning up. We'll get to that later.

'Oh, and see that a guard is detailed for the hatch, if you please,' he called to the retreating figure.

'Well, now – let's get down to business. How much do you know about this meeting, Dr. Keilty?' The admiral's jovial back-country manner was suddenly gone and in its place was that of the sailor who had come through the North Atlantic Convoys.

'Not much,' Keilty answered carefully, studying the admiral's face. 'Only what Admiral Rawingson told me yesterday afternoon. As I understand it, this business is not entirely over yet.'

'Very perceptive, Doctor, and I'm afraid you are right. You have met both Mr. Hutchins and Mr. Hallan? Good.' He leaned forward in his chair to rest his arms on the table, broad blunt-fingered hands, palms down. 'In a word, Doctor, although the Vietnamese no longer have that particular bomb, they are thought to have as many as four more.'

'I see,' Keilty said. 'That's nice. But that would seem to be *your* problem, wouldn't it?' Keilty leaned forward, placing his hands also on the table, staring straight at the admiral. The cabin was silent for a moment. Keilty could hear the noon cannon being fired, even through the sealed porthole. Someone shifted his chair and the noise broke the spell.

Without changing his position, the admiral abruptly switched the subject. 'Have you seen your porpoise today, Doctor?'

'Dolphin, Admiral. No, I haven't,' he answered wearily.

'You see, Doctor,' the admiral again changed the subject, 'it is possible that at least one more of these bombs is in the area of the straits, perhaps in a submarine.'

Keilty regarded the admiral steadily.

'It seems that at least two submarines were sold to the South Vienamese government during the war, one by the United States and the other by Australia. One was completely destroyed by loyal ARVN officers just before Saigon capitulated but they were not as successful with the second. It was sunk at its mooring but we know it was successfully raised and repaired. So, it seems there is a bit more to what is going on than we thought.

'We now know that they actually had formulated a many-stepped plan. Step one was initiated six days ago with the attack on Thailand. Following their usual pattern – an attack and then a quiet withdrawal, almost a probing action – they again have pulled back their troops within their borders. However, intelligence tells us they are continuing their massive build-up along the Thai-Laotian border. Step two was to be the bombing of the straits fleet – a second Pearl Harbor, in other words. But, thanks to you and your finny friend, that failed. But make no mistake, they have us out-maneuvered and they know it.'

'The same old story, then. They raise a flap and we run around like chickens,' Keilty interjected sarcastically.

'Oh, but not this time,' General Phillips put in. 'We have been keeping track of certain shipments of guided missiles out of eastern Europe. Six shipments have gone in the past seven months, four to India and two to Hanoi. The two shipments to Hanoi contained tactical short range missiles capable of eleven hundred miles with a payload of 600 pounds. Just sufficient for a nuclear device. They were originally intended to carry non-nuclear warheads in which case the range is normally around five hundred miles.'

'That's a tactical weapon,' Keilty snorted.

Phillips ignored the comment. 'As it now stands, we are pretty certain that at least four of these missiles are now aboard that rebuilt submarine. A group of Soviet technicians left Odessa four months ago and haven't been seen since. They were specialists in underwater-launched missiles. We believe that submarine has been modified to fire from depth. Somewhere in the South China Sea that sub is hiding and it probably is not too far away from the straits. And if it is, and if it is armed with those missiles . . .' he let the sentence trail off.

'Why near the straits? If they have a thousand mile range they could be anywhere between the Chinese coast and Australia.'

Phillips shook his head. 'No, we think they must be near the station. The Vietnamese do not have the sophisticated communications equipment to keep the sub informed of what is going on. She probably has to surface periodically and to keep the radio traffic from being picked up and giving her away, she would have to be close by and using low power, high frequency radio.'

'It seems,' Keilty said slowly, and with great resignation, 'that the last time I was informed what these crazy people were up to, I almost got my head shot off . . .

'Wait, don't tell me,' he held up his hand to forestall the admiral. 'I know, now, what this meeting is all about. You want me to persuade Charlie to help you find this submarine, right?'

When both Phillips and Collins nodded, he smiled sweetly and went on, 'This is an extremely important mission. The Reds must not be allowed to gain control of Southeast Asia, because do I know how valuable this part of the world is to the Free World? Why, when the Japanese took Singapore in the last war, do I realize, et cetera? Yes, I do. Of course I do, so let's skip the propaganda and build-up, right? That sub is somewhere off the coast of Sumatra and you want me to find . . . Charlie to find it, right?'

'I told you, gentlemen,' Rawingson laughed. 'Didn't I?'

Keilty glared at the rear admiral.

'SEATO has asked that you co-operate with us in this matter, Doctor. There is something going on out there that is obviously bigger than we had thought,' said General Phillips.

'Obviously,' Keilty muttered. He slumped back into the chair and regarded the gray overhead, festooned with pipes and cables worked with cryptic messages. The far bulkhead, fronting on the interior of the bridge, contained nothing but a hatchway and several prints – in very good taste – of rather well-known paintings. Keilty stared at Gauguin's painting of a Tahitian mountain rising from yellowed fields in reddish eminence, dwarfing the single figure trudging along a dusty road.

'Well, General, I am a civilian. And there would be a fee involved – payable in advance.'

'What?' Phillips exclaimed. He pushed back his chair and dropped his hands to his knees. 'You know the background of this . . . this plot, yet you make it contingent upon a fee? How the hell . . . ?'

'Pay the fee, General,' Rawingson said dryly.

'In advance – from the Department of Defense, and I want to see a cable from my bank before I move.'

'I'll be damned . . .'

'Pay the fee, General. I don't blame him a bit,' Rawingson said again. 'DOD can settle with SEATO later.'

Out of the corner of his eye, Keilty could see that the others were regarding him quizzically, and he grinned carefully at Phillips.

'I'll be damned . . .' Phillips ejaculated again. He then stood up. At the hatch, he turned to stare at Keilty, who did not even turn around. When the hatch slammed shut, both Keilty and Rawingson laughed uproariously.

The meeting dragged on into the late afternoon. Keilty was briefed on the situation by both Hallan and Hutchins. The two had been working together steadily for the past few years since Saigon and with it all of South Vietnam and later Cambodia had fallen to the Communists. Between them, they had amassed an immense amount of data.

Hutchins had specialized in the Vietnamese armed forces. The Vietnamese navy consisted in the main of a conglomeration of outdated craft; former South Vietnamese riverine and coastal patrol craft, six destroyers – two of them lately purchased from the Soviet Union – and three mine sweepers. The rest were miscellaneous vintage French and American motor torpedo boats. Their air force again was built mainly on French equipment – mostly propeller driven left over from the colonial days and more up-to-date captured American F-5's and helicopters and some new Migs, again from the Soviet Union and lately brought south from bases around Hanoi. The biggest addition had been the new SAM series of anti-aircraft missiles and ground facilities.

'Militarily,' Hallan finished up, 'they really have us as far as defending their turf goes. Outside their boundaries, nothing. I think we could probably talk the Malaysians and Indonesians into dealing with them alone but for the fact that they seem to be playing with a heavy hand. You just can't persuade anyone to argue with nuclear missiles.'

Keilty sat silently, chewing on his knuckle and staring at the Gauguin. He was beginning to feel a little homesick for his peaceful Key, and Margaritta – especially Margaritta.

Silently he cursed Rawingson for dragging him into this mess to begin with.

'So,' he growled, 'where does the submarine come in?'

'That's what we would like to know,' Hutchins answered sardonically. 'I doubt if there are thirty people in the entire Vietnamese Government and military establishment who know that it is there.' He paused a moment to stare at the backs of his hands. 'Perhaps they feel backed into a corner or maybe they still figure they can pull it out. The Vietnamese have never given a damn for quote, world opinion, unquote. They know they can always twist their underdog position around to justify just about any action they decide to undertake.'

'Hell, it doesn't stand to reason,' Keilty interrupted, 'that they will use the bombs on Singapore. The island will be absolutely no use to them if it's a mass of radioactive rubble. They need the naval yard, the airfields, the launching and harbor facilities, and most of the trade.'

'Precisely,' Collins put in. 'My own feeling in the matter is that they will use one or two of the bombs to create the tidal wave, still, in the strait. It would certainly be a lot easier for them than if they had to fight it out with our fleet to clear the channel. And there is only an even chance they would win. Either that . . .' And he paused for effect. '. . . or they will use them to threaten our allies in this area – nuclear blackmail, in other words.'

A knock sounded on the hatch, and Phillips stepped into the cabin and resumed his seat.

'Damned nonsense. I had to speak to the Joint Chiefs to get your advance fee paid, but you will have it tomorrow. Now, how much?'

'Two hundred thousand,' Keilty stated flatly. Phillips reddened, but Rawingson said mildly, 'Pay it.'

'You'll get the cable tomorrow,' Phillips choked.

'Fine,' Keilty said. 'Then we can *continue* tomorrow.'

Keilty said good-bye to Rawingson at the end of the gangway and walked slowly along the pier to the gate. The gray and blue camouflage of the *Vigilant* towered over him, bristling with uncovered, action-ready antiaircraft guns. Keilty stopped to stare at the cruiser, noting the covered cylindrical shapes of guided missiles and launchers where the four main turrets had once been located. She looked sleek and deadly.

He was passed through the gate, and pushed his way through

the crowds of Australian sailors waiting for rides into the city. The cab drew up in front of the U.S. Military Mission and Keilty, well known by now, was ushered right in by the marine guards. He wandered down the hall to the swimming pool, nodded to the guard, and walked in.

His footsteps echoed from the high brick walls as he walked to the edge of the pool's deep end. The pool was twelve feet deep and nearly fifty meters long, lined with white tile. Like the building, it had been constructed before the war in the mid-thirties, and bore the unmistakable stamp of that period's British military architecture.

Keilty sat down on the lowest row of the bleacher seats that lined the two long walls. Charlie, lying comfortably near the bottom, was completely engrossed in a TV program. Through the shimmering water, Keilty could see that it was one of the soap operas, piped in by satellite from Honolulu for the edification of military wives in the Southeast Asian area.

He watched the dolphin for a few moments, rising and sinking slowly in front of the plastic-boxed receiver. Finally he tossed a quarter into the water, directly above Charlie. The dolphin snapped around and shot to the surface, catching the falling quarter in his beak as he did so. He broke the surface, saw Keilty, and swam over to the edge of the pool and tossed the quarter to him.

Keilty pocketed the coin, and grinning, hooked up the transphonemator resting on the diving board.

'Hi, boss,' Charlie grinned, showing double rows of wolfish teeth.

'Hi, yourself. What've you been doing?'

Charlie backed off and jumped half onto the sloping edge that had been rigged for him.

'Not too much of anything. What the devil can you do in a lousy swimming pool? Say, did you know they have Jack LaLane out here?'

'Figures,' Keilty said. 'So they . . .'

'I found out that I'm getting fat. According to Jack LaLane, if you sit around doing nothing all day with no exercise, you're not going to burn up carbohydrates, and carbohydrates turn into fat.'

'Dolphins don't sit,' Keilty reminded him. He hunched down next to the pool. 'If it's getting fat you're worried about, I have just the thing in mind that will trim you down to a slim torpedo shape again. How about that?'

'How about what?' The dolphin's voice coming through the transphonemator had a distinctly suspicious tone to it. 'What's this one going to be, another wild adventure? When the hell do we go home, anyway?'

'What do you mean, go home? All you're worried about is that plane ride.'

'So?'

'So this. The big boys are in trouble again and it seems they need our help.'

'More bombs, I bet.' Charlie looked up at Keilty, staring directly into his eyes. Keilty was slowly learning to read the dolphin's expressions, but this one puzzled him.

'What's the matter?' he asked.

'I thought that we already helped them twice. They said that if we found the bomb for them, we could go back and they would leave us alone.'

'So they did, and we still can, but it looks as if the job was only half done. If we finish it, it means a heck of a lot of money, and with it, we can really get things rolling.'

The dolphin looked slightly puzzled. 'How do you mean half finished? I found the bomb for them all right, didn't I?'

'Yep. But they have more than one. There is a submarine somewhere out there.' He lowered his voice carefully. 'It's loaded with four guided missiles with nuclear bombs in them, and they want us to help them find it.'

Charlie slid halfway back into the water and slapped his tail. 'Is that all?' he almost chuckled. 'Why didn't you say so. There's no problem there.'

'No problem, what the devil are you talking about? Do you realize how much water there is . . . ?'

'Wait,' Charlie interrupted. 'I said it would be no problem because I know where the submarine is.'

Keilty almost fell off his heels in surprise. 'What?' he shouted. 'Where, for God's sake? How come you didn't tell me about it before?'

Charlie looked somewhat sheepish – no mean trick for a dolphin. 'I forgot. It was on the way back from the station. I was taking a last look round and I spotted something at the base of one of the islands. It took me a while to figure out what it was, but I'm sure it's a submarine.'

Keilty stood up and paced back and forth along the edge of the pool for several minutes, hands in his pockets and shoulders hunched in concentration. Finally he settled back down by the microphone. Charlie, who had been keeping pace with him, flopped back on the board.

'It could be a sub or even a surface ship sunk in the last war.' He paused for a while. 'Can you describe it?' he asked finally.

'Not too well. I had only a three-quarter view. It looked like a submarine that I had once seen, and it was resting on the bottom, perfectly upright.'

Keilty listened to the whirring of the transphonemator, staring absent-mindedly at the dolphin all the while. 'It could be,' he said finally. 'It's more than worth checking out anyway – do you think you can find it again?'

Charlie answered slowly, 'Of course, only . . .'

'Only what?' Keilty prompted. The dolphin said nothing, staring down at the board beneath his head. Finally he raised his head and looked at Keilty. 'Will this be the last time?'

Keilty saw what was troubling him and suddenly felt ashamed. He patted the dolphin's rough, bony head.

'This whole fiasco has been pretty rough on you, hasn't it?' He paused, searching for the right words.

'Look, Charlie, don't feel that you have to do this. Say no, and I'll tell them to go find their own God-damned submarine.' He stopped, at a loss to say more. He knew exactly what Charlie was feeling, or at least thought he did. Charlie had not wanted to become involved in human affairs, political or otherwise. The close bond *was* between the dolphin and himself, not between the dolphin and the West, or the human race, or any other part of it, but with him only. He refused to put it on the basis of a personal favor again. While he crouched on the edge of the pool, stroking the dolphin's sand-papery flank, he determined to say *no* flatly if Charlie refused. Charlie and he were not on terms of master and servant. Keilty considered Charlie as much a personal friend as he considered Weston a personal friend, and he was damned if he would change that relationship for anything.

The dolphin quivered slightly under his hand and slowly let his nine-and-a-half-foot length slide back into the pool.

'Aw, what the hell?' he said suddenly. 'If it will get me out of this tank, let's do it.'

'Thanks, Charlie,' Keilty said sincerely. 'Now, where is that sub?'

CHAPTER NINE

It was after 6 p.m. before Keilty got back to the hotel. He threaded his way through the crowds of people – a good many of them in the uniform of one country or another – filling the lobby. He waited impatiently for the elevator. The hotel's air conditioning was hard put to keep up with the humid heat of the pre-monsoon season, and even in his light clothes, he was wringing wet. All he wanted was a cool shower, a cold drink, dinner, and bed.

The elevator doors glided open softly and he stepped inside. 'Nine,' he said to the boy at the controls, and the doors closed softly. He leaned back against the plastic-walnut paneling and closed his eyes gratefully for a moment. When he opened them, he found he was staring into the dark muzzle of a 9 mm Walther. The muzzle was close enough for him to see the rifling grooves inside the barrel. He stood stock still, not changing his position an inch, except for the movement of his eyes.

The elevator boy had turned his back and was carefully examining the Otis Elevator sign. Behind the gun was a man with Chinese features – less than thirty, he judged – wearing a green uniform with a tag reading Wan Fin Delivery Service. Directly behind him, with a pistol pointing at Keilty's midriff, was an older man – a Caucasian, he thought, and then realized the man was probably Eurasian.

For a long moment they said nothing. The elevator passed the third floor.

'Don't you think this is overdoing it,' Keilty asked, the attempt at humor not quite coming off, as his mouth was suddenly dry.

'How is that?' the Eurasian asked politely.

'Pointing a gun at my face in a Singapore elevator.' Keilty tried to grin, but that didn't work either.

'I see,' the other answered. 'Well, perhaps Alan Ladd will appear on the scene. I am sure that if we were Japanese, he would.' The man smiled again, then his face tightened almost imperceptibly. 'Please do not make a move. We would be very sorry to have to kill you.'

The elevator stopped at the ninth floor and both men put their guns out of sight, the man in the delivery uniform shoving his in a jacket pocket. The doors slid aside and a neatly dressed couple stepped in. British tourists, from the way they were dressed in formal evening clothes. The Eurasian nodded to the blonde woman and her escort, saying 'Good evening.' He stepped out of the elevator and Keilty followed, the uniform right behind him. They walked down the blue-carpeted hall to Keilty's suite.

'What a shame,' Keilty said. 'Forgot to pick up my key at the desk.'

'Don't worry.' The Eurasian produced a passkey. He unlocked the door and Keilty was pushed inside.

He spun around, but both guns were on him instantly and he straightened slowly from his crouch.

'I wouldn't advise you . . .'

A muffled 'Ohh . . .' sounded from the door leading into the bedroom. The three men looked around to see a lovely Chinese girl clutch a short kimono to herself and stare at them with wide eyes. She saw the guns and tried to step back out of the doorway. A sharp word in Chinese stopped her, and she came slowly out of the bedroom.

Keilty rolled his eyes up in supplication and sat down on the edge of a bookcase. The girl was his date from the night before. He watched her cross the room hesitatingly, long legs shown to good advantage beneath the kimono which did nothing to hide a beautiful figure. Her hair, hanging shoulder length and cut evenly across the back, matched almost perfectly the muted brown of her almond-shaped eyes.

She stared at him in fright and he spread his hands in helplessness.

'A complication, a very bad complication,' the Eurasian rasped. The Chinese gunman fired a question at her in Chinese and she answered slowly, then bit off a single word. He was across the room in two steps and slapped her hard on the face. The blow cracked like a pistol shot. Keilty lunged off the bookcase and caught the Eurasian's gun butt behind the ear before he had taken a step. He went down hard, his head a mass of exploding lights.

Through the haze that swirled in his head, he could hear questions being put to the girl in Chinese. He tried to get to his knees, but the blow on the head seemed to have drained his strength completely. There were more slaps and muffled screams. Then he felt hands go under his arms, lifting him into a chair.

His head was beginning to clear somewhat. He opened his eyes and the room swam sickeningly for a moment. Keilty finally managed to focus his eyes on the figure of the Eurasian, perched on the arm of the couch. Keilty noticed that the Eurasian had attached a silencer to his .38 S&W Police Special.

He heard a slap and turned to see the Chinese girl lying on the floor, face cradled in her arms.

'Tell your bully boy,' Keilty said dangerously, 'that if he touches her once more, I'll break his back.'

'Your heroics are a bit late,' the other laughed. 'We are already quite finished with her.' Keilty did not like the emphasis on the 'quite finished'.

'Who is she?' the Eurasian asked.

Keilty put a hand to the side of his head, gingerly massaging the spot where the gun had struck him. 'She's a friend.'

'Her name, please?'

'Why?'

'Curiosity, more than anything else. She is a complication as I said before. I would like to know her name.'

Keilty glanced at her, still lying on the rug. She raised her head to look at him, and he could see the red marks of the slaps and a darkening bruise at the outer edge of her left eye. There were no traces of tears. She was frightened but trying desperately not to show it. He smiled at her, then shifted his glance to the Chinese with the Walther. The man said nothing, but his eyes said it for him. The Chinese smiled and rubbed his hand along the stubby barrel.

'Her name is Tina,' he said, turning back to the Eurasian.

'Her last name, please.'

'I don't know,' Keilty answered. 'We only met last night.'

'I see,' thoughtfully. He brought the gun to bear directly on Keilty's face.

'Her last name,' he said harshly.

Keilty stared at the muzzle and burst into laughter. 'You stupid jerk. You kidnap me in an elevator, haul me in here, find her, then threaten to shoot me if I don't tell you the last name of a girl I only met last night. You don't expect me to believe that, do you?'

The Eurasian grinned sheepishly. 'No, I don't. You are more intelligent than you appear, Dr. Keilty, in spite of the Ph.D. following your name.'

'So, you know my name.'

'Yes we do. We know quite a bit about you, in fact . . .' The telephone buzzed softly and he picked it up, listened for a moment, then said, 'Five minutes,' and hung up.

'Get her clothes,' he said to the Chinese. Then to Keilty, 'We are going to take a short taxi ride. I am sure that you will find yourself treated as an honored guest when we arrive . . . if you co-operate.'

The Chinese came back into the room and dumped an arm-load of feminine clothing on the floor next to the girl. He spoke harshly in Chinese and stepped back as she got gracefully to her feet and began to slip into the clothes. He turned away, grimacing, to cover Keilty while the Eurasian quietly watched the girl dress. Keilty laughed shortly at the Chinese and laughed louder when he stepped forward, face an angry red.

The Eurasian handed Tina a comb, an unexpected gesture, until Keilty realized it might attract attention if they went through the lobby with her hair awry. It would be bad enough with the swelling eye. The Eurasian stepped into the bedroom and came back with her purse. He opened it and dumped its contents on the table, and tossed her compact to her.

'My, my, how dangerous.' He held up a black-handled tube and touched a stud. A stiletto-thin blade sprang forward with a quiet swish. He placed the tip of the blade against the coffee table glass, shoved it back into the handle, and pocketed the knife. The purse held nothing else but the usual make-up, scarf, money, etc., and he shoved the contents back into the bag and tossed it across the room to her.

'Now listen to me, both of you,' he said, his voice harsh. 'We are going down to the lobby and into the first cab at the head of the line. My associate here will go ahead of us and wait at the front doors until we have gone through. He will follow in the second cab.

'You, Dr. Keilty, will take, ah . . . Tina's left arm, and I, her right. You are both to smile and make small talk.

'And, Dr. Keilty, please do not think that you are so valuable to us that we would hesitate to shoot you – and of course, first we shall kill the young lady. Do you understand?'

Keilty nodded and the Eurasian motioned the Chinese out. He went with a backward glance of pure hatred at Keilty, and the door closed softly.

The Eurasian noticed. 'I would not advise riding Mr. Lee, Dr. Keilty. He is a pathological killer. He obeys me only because I control his heroin supply.' He motioned Keilty to his feet and slipped the gun into his jacket pocket. With his hand in the pocket, it looked completely normal, no more bulge than his hand would normally have caused. A real professional, Keilty thought.

He took Tina's hand and put it under his arm, giving it a brief squeeze. She smiled weakly, but the fear was still large in her eyes.

They waited for the elevator, and when it came, the same boy was still at the controls. He paid them no more attention than he would to a normal passenger. Keilty was thoughtful all the way down.

They walked into the spacious modern lobby, full of elegantly styled Danish furniture, and cheerily carpeted with a deep gold rug.

Keilty caught sight of the Chinese, standing at the Pan American reservations counter, talking with a clerk and apparently paying the three no attention. Keilty paused, but the Eurasian dropped Tina's right arm and stepped away. 'Don't try anything, Dr. Keilty. Look over there by the cigarette counter.'

Keilty glanced over. Two men, Chinese, were standing together, apparently deep in conversation. They were well dressed and appeared to be businessmen, but the one facing them was staring past the other's shoulder – at them.

'In the lobby of the Hilton?'

'Yes, Dr. Keilty. You and the young lady will both be dead, and I will be gone before you drop to the floor.'

'Not very valuable, am I?' he said, glancing around. He felt Tina's hand tighten on his arm.

'On the contrary, you are more valuable to us alive. But, if we have to kill you, well . . .'

'Okay, I see your point.'

They walked forward to the doors, and the Chinese gunman, just turning away from the Pan Am counter, held open the door for them and stopped just outside and lit a cigarette as they went down the broad steps and climbed into the cab that came up to meet them. The cab drove off, and as they rounded the curb towards the boulevard, Keilty could see the Chinese getting into another cab. He settled back, wondering what the devil was next. The Eurasian had his gun out and was sitting with his back to the door, the gun steady against the girl's side. The cab driver, peering into the rear-view mirror from time to time, held the cab to the speed limit. He headed down the boulevard to the main part of the city, expertly dodging other cabs, cars, and pedestrians.

At a stoplight, Keilty had a chance to look around at the brilliantly lit main section of Singapore. The city had surprised him with its cleanliness. The streets were scrubbed down by water trucks early every morning and an army of sweepers kept the streets spotless during the day. Lining either side of the boulevard as far as he could see were Western-style shops lit with neon, making it look more like London or New York than one of the largest cities in the Orient.

The cab started forward again and the girl huddled closer. Instinctively he put his arm around her shoulder, and the gun muzzle jammed into his ribs. He stiffened.

'Do not do that again,' the Eurasian hissed. 'Remove your arm.'

The cab driver leaned back to say something at the same time, and the Eurasian bent slightly forward to hear, just as the girl moved her shoulder.

Keilty, almost without thinking, shoved the girl with his right arm, pushing the pistol forward. The gun went off and the bullet whipped through a fold of his shirt. He grabbed the gun with his left hand and twisted. The girl leaning forward on the Eurasian's arm hampered his movements long enough for Keilty to uncock a vicious short right against his ear.

The pistol came loose. He reversed it and fired point-blank into the white face, then he jammed the gun against the driver's neck.

'Keep driving,' he said steadily, 'or you'll lose the back of your head.' He glanced quickly at the Eurasian lying slumped almost to the floor. A thin trickle of blood gleamed from the bullet hole under his left eye. Keilty pulled Tina back into the seat with his free hand and gave her a brief grin.

Leaning forward, 'Do you speak English?'

The driver shrugged and glanced into the mirror. Keilty took a quick look out the back window. The second cab had dropped back a bit and was now pulling around to fall in behind. The driver slowed for the stoplight ahead and Keilty rolled down the side window.

'Tina, tell him to pull over to the outside lane and stop for the light.'

The girl leaned forward and repeated in Chinese. Keilty jammed the muzzle against his head again.

'He will do it. I told him you would kill him quickly if he didn't.'

'Good girl.' He bent over her and found the knife in the dead man's pocket.

The cab drew up to the left, and as Keilty had hoped, the other cab stopped beside them. He pressed the girl down into the seat and huddled back against the door frame. The Chinese peered over, startled at the apparently empty back seat, and pulled the door of his cab open, gun in hand.

Keilty leaned forward and shot him twice. He was halfway out of the cab, gun partly raised. The expression of disbelief washing over his face stopped instantly. His hand opened and the gun dropped from it. He folded after it.

'Move! ' Keilty yelled, and the driver jammed the accelerator, screaming around the corner, narrowly missing a large military truck. The cab shot down the street and around a second corner. Ahead, the street emptied into Raffles Square, the center of metropolitan Singapore. Keilty had the driver skirt the northern edge of the square, then drive off onto a side street and from there back onto a narrow avenue one block from the boulevard. The cab pulled up to the curb, facing the main rear entrance to a large department store.

Keilty clubbed the driver at the base of the skull and ripped the microphone loose from the dashboard. They got out of the cab and walked into the store as if they were ordinary shoppers. As the glass doors swung shut, Keilty saw another cab pull up and the two Chinese from the hotel cigarette counter get out. They looked up and down the street, then entered the store quickly, one going to a pay phone just inside the door.

'Trouble followeth,' Keilty grinned at the girl. 'Think you can stand a little fast walking?'

Tina stared up at him; she barely came up to his shoulders. Her brown eyes were wide and still full of fear but she smiled tremblingly and squeezed his hand.

'Good girl.' They hurried down the main aisle, Keilty looking for another entrance besides the front. They moved quickly between the various counters. He pulled the girl aside quietly, stepping back into a row of high bookracks. A Chinese, neatly dressed in a dark suit, stepped through the main doors and stood to one side, glancing around the store. Keilty risked a quick look behind, but couldn't spot the two following in the press of people in the store.

From somewhere above came the soft chiming of bells, and Keilty looked at his watch – five to nine.

'The store closes at nine o'clock,' the girl whispered. 'Perhaps we can mix with the people leaving.'

'No,' he replied. 'That's just what they will expect us to do.' He studied the man at the door for a moment. 'Look, you start towards the door. They'll be looking for us together, and know what I look like. But they don't know you. There's a drugstore just up the street. Wait for me there.'

Before she could protest, he pushed her out into the aisle and stepped back quickly around the bookshelf.

Tina went slowly towards the door, pausing to examine a display of jewelry, then walked past the Chinese at the door.

He looked at her, then made as if to step in front of her, but Keilty, head down and walking fast, came into view around the other side of the shelf. The Chinese stepped back and reached inside his jacket. The gun in Keilty's hand came up quickly from where it was hidden in back of his leg, and popped once.

The girl had already disappeared as Keilty ran past the falling body and pushed through the door. Once in the street, he turned left and walked fast towards the drugstore, keeping to the inside of the wall. A green American car went past him and stopped in front of the department store and several men got out.

The drugstore was half a block up the street and Keilty was inside minutes later. Tina was waiting for him at the magazine rack. Keilty moved casually to the other side, carefully searching the shop. The drugstore looked better suited to a large midwestern shopping center. Highly modern, full of gleaming plastic and steel. Even the bottles and lotions in the women's make-up section were the familiar shapes and brands. Satisfied that he hadn't been followed, Keilty moved around next to Tina.

'So far so good. But it won't take them long to get onto us. Is there any other way out than the front?'

'Yes,' Tina nodded almost imperceptibly. With the magazine, she indicated a narrow corridor leading back past the pharmacist's counter.

Keilty grasped her arm and steered her to the back of the store. As they started past the counter, a Malay in a white jacket stepped out of a side door, and surprised, stopped.

'I am very sorry, sir,' he smiled politely, 'but this area is for staff only.'

'Fine.' Keilty stepped forward, pressing the gun into the man's stomach. 'Let's go, hurry!'

The man gasped, his face paling at the sight of the silencer-stubbed automatic. Keilty leaned on the gun and he retreated. They passed a door leading to an alleyway and Keilty grabbed his shoulder and pushed him through. The door led to a small alley that ended at the store entrance. Along the open sides, garbage cans were stacked against a wall. Parked against the drugstore wall was a white Volkswagen delivery truck with the name of the drugstore painted brightly in English, Malay, and Chinese.

Keilty glanced quickly through the doorway and clubbed the druggist with the pistol. He went down without a sound. Tina turned away as Keilty dragged him into a shadowed corner, then moved quickly to the end of the short alley. The entrance to the street was less than ten yards away and around that corner the avenue opened up, running down past the department store and ending at the square. Keilty could see two cars parked at the entrance and several men waiting outside the doors. A third car stopped opposite the store and three men got out and hurried across the almost empty street.

Keilty beat it back to Tina and hustled her inside the unlocked delivery truck. The keys were not in the ignition, and swearing, he jumped out again and dug through the unconscious druggist's pockets. He found a set of keys, but none with the circular Volkswagen crest. The druggist was beginning to come around and he left him.

Tina, sitting in the other seat, looked at him with a white face as he slid into the driver's seat and ducked his head under the narrow dash.

With her knife, taken from the Eurasian's pocket, he sliced the insulation off one side of the two ignition wires.

'I hope to hell this works,' he muttered. 'I've never hot-wired a Volkswagen before.' He straightened, pressed the wires together, and the engine caught immediately.

The VW moved down the alley and turned into the street. When they turned onto the boulevard, Keilty breathed a deep sigh of relief.

He slid into the traffic stream, moving with it for several blocks, then pulled the truck over to the curb, into an empty parking space, and stopped.

'End of the line,' he announced gaily. 'Let's dump this thing before we have the police after us as well.'

He hopped out and came around to open the door and help Tina out. They walked down the street a ways, Tina almost running to keep up with his long strides. They passed several cabs, but all seemed to be driven by Chinese.

'For God's sake,' he complained, 'don't they have any Malay cab drivers around here?'

'You don't think that the Communists have all the taxi drivers organized do you?' The girl laughed for the first time that evening.

'I don't know, but we're not going to try and find out,' he said grimly. 'We've got to get off the street pretty soon, before they find us again.'

'Why are they after you? Are you a policeman of some kind?'

Keilty laughed quietly, turning to peer back up the street. 'That's the last thing in the world I am, pussycat. What makes you think that?'

'Do you know who those men were who took us from your hotel room?'

'Sure, Communists.'

'Yes, they were,' she said. Tina stopped and turned to face him. 'But they were more than that. The one who beat me told me who he was to frighten me. I was only a small child after the war, but I remember the power and the terror of the Chinese secret societies after the Japanese left. The British took a long time to stop them. The one who slapped me was a member of the Canton Tong. You have heard of it?'

Keilty grinned at her. 'Tong-war stuff; I thought the Reds cleaned them out when they took China . . .'

'No,' Tina interrupted. 'They turned them to their own use. They are not Communists as much as they are gangsters doing the Communists' dirty work, and they are used in Singapore only when they want someone very badly. Now they are only gansters and work for whoever will pay them.'

'So. Things are beginning to clear up a little,' Keilty said thoughtfully. 'Well, this is your town – how do you suggest we get safe transportation? We can't go back to the hotel tonight . . . but there is somewhere that we can go and we had better go fast.'

'You have the gun?' Tina said quietly. 'We can still take a cab.'

Keilty laughed again, kissed her quickly, and started walking to the cab stand ahead.

'How do you know so much about the tong?'

'Every Chinese knows about the tong . . . and my parents still live in Canton. I visited them two years ago.'

They came up to the cab stand and slid quickly into the first cab.

'Hotel Metropoli,' Keilty said, leaning across the seat, 'and don't touch that radio.' He pressed the gun into the driver's neck. 'Move.'

Keilty banged on Rawingson's door loudly, then banged again. He heard shuffling, the click of a lamp going on, and muffled curses. The door opened a crack, then Rawingson pulled it all the way open.

'What the hell are you doing here . . . ?'

Keilty pushed in and swung the door shut quickly.

'Howdy, Pete, bed so early?'

Rawingson wrapped his robe more tightly around him and planted his hands on his hips. 'What are you up to . . . ?'

'Never mind the small talk. We've got some pretty bad trouble.' Keilty flopped down on the couch, pulling Tina after him. She huddled into his arm and stared at the imposing figure of the white-haired admiral.

'First of all, pick up that phone and get some marine guards up here, fast.'

Rawingson, face incredulous, started to protest, but Keilty cut him off. 'We were kidnapped from my hotel tonight about seven – by the Communists.'

'What the hell!' Rawingson exploded. He didn't waste time in questions or disbelief, but crossed the room. The phone rang just as he reached to pick it up. He answered and listened for a moment, his face screwing up into a frown.

'All right, keep it quiet. Not a word to anyone, or else. I have him here right now. Tell Commander Peterson I want the guard doubled around the building and I want four armed marines here at my suite in plain clothes – five minutes. No,' he said crossly, 'I'll explain to him later.' Rawingson hung up, opened the drawer and took out a .45 Colt automatic, checked the clip and dropped it into the pocket of his kimono.

He took the chair across the room and stared at the two on the couch.

'That was Operations. They just got a call from the consul's office. There is a warrant out for your arrest. Car theft and assault with a deadly weapon. What the hell's going on?'

Keilty laughed and crossed the room to the bar and mixed three stiff drinks. 'That, my friend, is a mighty long story.'

Briefly, Keilty ran through the events of the past hours. 'So, Pete, there is either a leak somewhere, or else they want to get their hands on both Charlie and me.'

'Huumph,' Rawingson snorted. 'Just you would be enough. Plenty of dolphins around.' He drained the glass and stared out the broad window morosely. 'The only night I get a chance to get to bed early, and you have to come banging in here with some wild tale and every comic-strip oriental bandit in hot pursuit.'

'They are not comic-strip bandits, Admiral, they are very dangerous men,' Tina said quietly from the couch.

'She's right, Pete. I've got a bullet hole to prove it.' He opened his jacket; his shirt was stained red where the bullet had grazed his side. Tina jumped from the couch and was across to the bathroom before he could say more.

While Tina cleaned the slight wound and bandaged it, Rawingson made some more phone calls. When he finished and hung up the phone, a knock sounded on the door. Both men were instantly on their feet, guns in hands. Keilty pushed Tina towards the bedroom.

'Yes,' Rawingson called.

'Sergeant Bennington, sir. Operations sent us.'

'Just a minute.' Rawingson went to the door, while Keilty stepped back into the alcove where he would have clear fire on the door. Rawingson opened it a crack, then flung it open all the way . . . and sighed when he saw that the faces were American. The sergeant saluted and showed his I.D. Rawingson positioned the marines: one to the lobby, one to the end of the hall, and the other two outside the door.

When the door closed behind them, Rawingson turned to Keilty. 'I've set up the meeting for seven hundred hours. It looks like we had better shift into high gear. The dolphin will be brought aboard and the *Vigilant* will sail immediately.' Keilty was about to tell him that Charlie already knew where the sub was, when Tina came back into the living room.

'I suggest,' Rawingson said, looking at the girl's worn face, 'that the young lady had better get some sleep.' He nodded at Keilty.

Keilty agreed and ushered the girl into the master bedroom. 'You're safe now, Tina,' he said quietly. 'Get undressed and get some sleep. I'll see that you're taken care of.'

She reached up and drew his head down, kissing him long and deeply, then leaned against him for a moment. He brushed her dark hair back out of her eyes and kissed her on the tip of the nose. 'Sleep, sweetheart, and don't worry.'

He came back out into the living room, where Rawingson had fresh drinks waiting. 'We're not waiting for tomorrow. I've got Hallan and Hutchins both coming in an hour – Washington wants us to move fast.

'Who is she?' He switched subjects abruptly.

'Who?'

'The girl,' Rawingson replied impatiently. 'Who is she and where did you meet her?'

Keilty grinned. 'Just a friend. I met her last night and she was waiting in my suite tonight when those thugs shoved me in the door. I told you.'

'Yes, but where did you pick her up is what I want to know.'

'I didn't. Not in that sense anyway. Peter Owterry, you remember him, the New Zealander . . .'

'Yes, go on.' Rawingson waved his hand impatiently.

'Anyway,' Keilty continued, looking reproachfully at the admiral, 'he introduced me to her and I took her out.'

'Had you made a date for tonight?'

'No, but . . .'

'That's what I thought. She goes into custody as soon as she wakes up.'

Keilty finished the drink. 'I was going to ask you to take care of her. It's for darned sure that she can't stay in Singapore.'

'Well, we'll take care of her for the time being and she'll be perfectly safe.'

The phone rang again and Rawingson picked it up. As he listened, his face turned red with rage. He swore furiously and slammed the phone down. Still swearing, he started to pace the room.

'Now what?' Keilty asked.

'They tried to break into the Military Mission building but they arrived just as the additional sentries came up.' Rawingson picked up the phone and dialed a number. 'They didn't get inside the building. Go tell the boys outside to pass Hallan and Hutchins through. We're leaving as soon as they get here.'

When Keilty returned, he found Rawingson on the phone again. Finally, he hung up and swung around. 'That was Honolulu. They said, move immediately.' He swore loudly, then calmed himself with visible effort. 'They want the sub found yesterday. But while finding it, we aren't supposed to let it know it's being hunted.'

'When you do find it, then what?'

'Correction, when *you* find it . . . remember that two hundred thousand. They say, destroy it immediately.'

Keilty grinned. 'In that case relax. Charlie already knows where it is.'

Rawingson was quiet for a long minute, then: 'I should expect anything else?' he said in a tired voice.

CHAPTER TEN

It was close to 3 a.m. when the five-ton truck wheeled up to the cargo stage, dimly lit by lights from the *Vigilant*'s bridge. Keilty came around to the gate just as the new steel semi-tank that had been built for Charlie was unloaded by a forklift. Keilty climbed onto the running board and directed the driver to the stage.

Keilty hooked the slings himself and patted Charlie's broad back. He climbed onto the tank step and shouted for the operator to lift them onto the ship. The slings came up taut and the tank lifted off the pier, swung free, and moved upwards slowly. The gray steel hull of the cruiser slipped past and they were level with, then above the rail. From his vantage point, Keilty could see the ring of marines in position at the end of and along the pier. A hastily mounted machine-gun emplacement faced the dock area at the end of the pier, and two large searchlights, dismounted from *Vigilant*'s bridge, illuminated the area with stark, white light. He ran his hand over Charlie's rough hide again to calm him. The dolphin lay half supported by the shallow water of the tank.

The winch moved them over the deck, past the battery of missiles, shrouded in canvas but pointing angrily to the sky as if straining at their mooring clamps to be released. The No. 2 ammunition hold yawned under them and they began the descent into the black maw. As they passed the hatch edge, several batteries of lamps flashed on, and the tank settled gently to the rubber-tired truck. Keilty jumped off and unfastened the chain with the aid of two ratings, and the slings were pulled out of the hold and the clamshell doors boomed shut above them. The hold was a large rectangular area, two decks deep, and was directly over the main magazine.

An electric tractor backed up; the hitch of the truck was snapped tight and it was towed away toward the hospital. Rawingson and Keilty had deemed this the safest place for the dolphin, deep in the interior of the ship, and Captain Whittlson had readily agreed. Keilty rode along as they passed down the wide steel corridors with their maze of brightly colored overhead pipes. The *Vigilant* was a fairly new ship, converted to missiles. She had been one of the last built in the Clyde shipyards in the early fifties, and she was built well. She was more spacious, faster, and better armored than her World War II predecessors. The hospital was a large double cabin amidship, below the water line, and extremely well equipped.

Keilty settled Charlie into one of the medical bays in the office and filled the tank, taking the strain off the dolphin's internal organs. He had already explained the situation to Charlie before taking him from the Military Mission pool. Charlie's first question had been about the gunfire he had heard. He didn't know what it was, but had guessed that it was something that might possibly harm him.

Keilty had patiently explained what had happened since he had left earlier that evening. He went into detail over the reasons for the kidnapping and told Charlie point-blank that it appeared that the Vietnamese had mounted the attack in an effort to kill him. He pointed out the desperation behind the attack – a handful of agents against a U.S. military post.

Charlie had slipped off the board without a word and had slowly coursed up and down the pool for several minutes before coming back to it.

'Why do they want to destroy me?' he had asked, puzzlement and hurt in his mechanical voice.

'Because they are scared,' Keilty answered point-blank. 'This whole business is as old as mankind. One group trying to force another to believe and act as they believe, and the other group resisting. Human history is composed of these ridiculous counter-marchings to and fro. And we are as guilty as the Communists. Less than thirty years ago, it was the Germans and the Japanese. The Germans, under the guise of National Socialism, trying to force other people in their part of the world to believe as they believed. They were so adamant about others accepting their beliefs that close to ten million people died. In this part of the world, the Japanese did it for the sake of Japanese aggrandizement and again millions more died. Now, they are our best allies.

'In the history of my country, the United States, it has happened four times in less than two hundred years – the War of Independence that "freed" us from England, the same country we are helping today; the Civil War, between two sections of our country; the Spanish-American War, because we believed that the people of a small island, Cuba, should be free to decide their own fate; and South Vietnam where we thought we were helping and stayed long past the time we were doing any good.'

Keilty paused and gazed morosely at his big hands. 'It all seems futile in the light of later events. Now we are dealing with weapons that can kill a million people at one relatively inexpensive blow. We've come a long ways, haven't we?

'But I believe that we are fighting for something that perhaps will make all this worthwhile – the idea that anyone is free to come and go, to earn his living and be happy without a collective government telling him what to do. Government is the worst and the best invention of man. It depends on how it is used. The Communists, broadly, want to use it to force people to live in a way that is completely unnatural to human beings. In a word, they actually believe in the innate goodness of human beings, which in a way is true. But humans are also very opportunistic and will take advantage of any situation that they can. Communism just will not work. But they believe it will. They believe they are right and we believe we are right. Trouble is,' he finished, 'I believe we are a little righter than they.'

When he finished, Charlie was silent, looking up at the hunched figure with troubled eyes. Keilty was again struck by the dolphin's humanness. The intelligence lying behind the black pupils. Charlie could feel the emotions that vied for expression, for mastery of the man, and suddenly he realized that Keilty was just as troubled, just as uncertain as he was. When he had realized this, he began to look at the man with new eyes. Keilty did not any more know for sure what was right than he did, but he was doing a job he felt had to be done. He fumbled for a moment for something that Jack had once told him. He hadn't understood then, but it was clear now. Jack had said that nothing was ever clearly black and white, that there were innumerable shades of gray between the extremes, and it was each man's own fate to decide which shade of gray he would adopt for his own. Some would believe they had picked the right hue; others would never be sure. The latter were the great ones, Jack had said. They did what they had to, never knowing if they were right or wrong, but doing it because they had made the choice.

And of a sudden, it was clear to him that earth was a very small planet. For thousands of years, man had been the dominant life form, only because he had intelligence and had no intelligent competition. But now, Charlie realized, his people were shortly to take their place, hopefully beside man, at man's insistence. They had to, or they would perish. Man was also moving into the sea. For a moment, pure terror washed through him at the thought. And for the rest of his life, this terror was never completely to leave him. Man could either be an enemy or a friend. But how to be a friend, unless they met man with a force equal to his? For man had always to dominate. It was engrained in his genes. Again the question: degenerate or advance? He knew that the answer must not be degenerate. He had already taken one step; he must take another. Somewhere in the infinity of mirror images was the answer he would need, he or another of his kind.

'I'll go,' he said simply.

Keilty nodded, rubbed his hand on Charlie's head, and then left. Ten minutes later in Rawingson's quarters, he was writing out a detailed message to Jack Weston, the gist of which was to gather up certain equipment and get over to Patrick Air Force Base as quick as he could.

At the same time, Rawingson was speaking urgently into a phone with a scrambled connection to Washington and Canberra and London.

Only Charlie felt the ship get under way. He lay in his tank, his great eyes unblinking.

CHAPTER ELEVEN

The helicopter carrying Jack Weston and the special equipment that Keilty had ordered rendezvoused with the cruiser north of Natuna Island. As the helicopter hovered over the square landing area on the afterdeck and settled down ponderously, the cruiser was already swinging around south in a tight circle that would bring them back to the Riouw Islands in a little over eighteen hours at thirty knots. The wake, Keilty noted, was already churning out swiftly behind them.

Jack jumped from the helicopter, and clutching his hat and ducking low, he scuttled to meet Keilty before the rotors had stopped. He carried a duffel bag in one hand, a heavy suitcase in the other.

Below, in the cruiser's wardroom, Weston sank gratefully into a padded armchair and abandoned himself to the bliss of air conditioning after the over 100° heat and 95 per cent humidity outside.

'Christ,' he said mildly, 'I thought I was never going to get here.'

'Fast trip?' Keilty inquired innocently.

Weston grunted. 'Fast! They had an F4F at Patrick AFB waiting to take me to Edwards and a RB-76 from there to Hawaii. Mid-air refueling over Guam and a destroyer at Singapore. The destroyer left Singapore like its tail was on fire just a few hours after you. A hundred miles or so southwest of here, they threw me into the helicopter and kicked us off. Twenty-eight hours and I lost track of the time changes.' He slumped wearily, utter dejection written all over his face.

Rawingson and Captain Whittlson came in to join them and shook hands with Weston.

'What's in the duffel bag?' Keilty asked.

'Ha. It's just chock-full of goodies. There's a crate on the helicopter that has your and Charlie's diving gear plus the other stuff you wanted.'

'Hey, wait . . .' Rawingson interrupted, 'yours and whose diving gear?' He looked from one to the other as if unable to decide whether or not his leg was being pulled.

Keilty grinned at Jack. 'Charlie's gear,' he chuckled.

Rawingson took out his pipe and stared abstractly into the

bowl. 'Okay, I give up. What you two birds pull no longer surprises me.' He looked up at Keilty patiently. 'Now, would you mind explaining to an old and very tired man exactly why that crazy fish . . . ah,' he held up a hand, '. . . I know, dolphin. Why that Charlie character should need breathing gear.'

The steward interrupted to wheel in a tray of drinks. Before the captain could finish explaining that he had ordered them because he felt their American visitor would need one, Jack was already thirstily coaching the British seaman on making his own version of the gin and tonic. The steward was aghast that Jack insisted he make it with lemon rather than lime.

Keilty turned back to Rawingson.

'How long can you stay underwater?' he asked.

'Absolute maximum?' Rawingson picked up his drink and sat down. 'Four minutes, I guess. Why?'

'Well,' Keilty answered, 'a dolphin can't stay under a heck of a lot longer – maybe ten minutes by stretching it. Don't forget, he's an air-breather and a mammal, just like you.'

'How could I forget it, for God's sake, you bring it up every chance you get. Anyway, how come?'

Keilty chuckled and went on. 'A dolphin's lungs are really not much bigger than yours, maybe a third or so. Charlie is nine and a half feet long and weighs three hundred and seventy-five pounds. His lung is a bit more efficient, although *relatively* it is about the same size. So he has maybe a three- to five-minute edge on you. Dolphins are coastal-water animals, rarely straying beyond the limits of the continental shelf. There isn't much in the open ocean in the way of food or in the deeper waters several miles off the edge of the shelf, except for bottom-dwelling animals and those in the upper currents. The mid-oceans are almost deserts, with the exception of the arctic and antarctic waters where temperature is a factor.

'Anyway, what I'm getting at is that Charlie needs air to stay underwater longer than ten minutes. So Jack and I rigged up a special self-contained underwater apparatus for him.'

'Why special? Can't he use the same type that a man uses, with maybe a different kind of mouthpiece?'

Jack finished mixing a second drink and brought it over to Rawingson.

'Not really, Admiral. Dolphins don't breathe through their mouths. There is no connection at the back of the throat to the trachea as in man. Otherwise, every time he opened his mouth, he'd get a lung full or stomach full of water.

'Dolphins breathe through the blowhole located on top and towards the back of their heads. So we had to come up with a special gadget that would seal him off without limiting his breathing while on the surface.'

'Which brings us to the next item of discussion,' Keilty interposed. 'Just how do you expect us to go about this business of finding one little dinky sub somewhere in the South China Sea?'

'You said that Charlie knew where it was,' Rawingson said accusingly.

Keilty snorted. 'I said that he said he saw something, and that that something looked like a submarine. Neither one of us can or will guarantee the validity of that statement.'

'Okay, okay,' Rawingson held up a hand. 'Anyway, I realize that there is no way of being sure it's still there. We haven't tried using any anti-submarine warfare techniques in case they would spot us and hightail it for home. Nobody knows that we know, except the four of us,' and he waved a hand to take them all in, 'Charlie, and the people you met in Singapore, and the general staff.'

'What about the kidnappers?' Keilty asked.

'Our people picked up the taxi driver and he turned out to be a member of the Singapore Communist Party – *distinct* Peking leanings. From documents found at their headquarters, the word to pick you up seemed to have come from Peking rather than from Moscow. The CIA claims it was just another one of their tries to get more information. Even if you had been taken, on which *they* only laid a fifty-fifty chance of success, you probably would have been dropped back at your hotel rooms the next night with no memory of anything except one hell of a good time in a brothel. Yet they would have picked your skull clean, then replaced the incident with happy thoughts.'

'They can do that?' Jack asked, his voice showing disbelief.

Rawingson nodded soberly. 'They can, and do.

'Hell!' Rawingson stood up and began pacing up and down the wardroom. 'People think that just because we don't fight a hot war, that everything is confined to words and oh-so-proper diplomatic meetings. Well it's not,' he said, swinging around to face Jack. 'Let me tell you.'

Jack grinned. 'I'm no military man. The Coast Guard is just glorified civil service. No one ever tells us anything. And you think you got problems.'

'Okay, okay, you two simmer down,' Keilty growled. 'I suspected it was something like that. If they had known what we were up to, they'd have gone after you as well, Admiral. The only thing that puzzles me is why they attacked the Mission building.'

'Same reason they went after you,' Rawingson replied. 'They had a truck and hoist around the corner. Our boys got there in time to see it disappear down the street. They never did catch it. They couldn't kill the dolphin by shooting it, because the first thing he would have done would be to go to the bottom. They could have poisoned him, but they didn't have any poison. Or they could have tossed some high explosive into the pool. But the only explosives they had, they used to blow down the gates. Like I said, they were paid by Peking, not Moscow.

Keilty snorted. 'Don't you know that the Russians have been interested in dolphins for years. And anything the Russians are interested in, the Red Chinese are too. They probably wanted to compare notes, Soviet-American notes, that is. It wasn't just plain old curiosity.'

Keilty slammed a meaty fist against the tabletop. 'For God's sake, what kind of intelligence system do you birds have? If I'd of known that you guys were such rank amateurs, we would have never signed to play on your team.'

'Well, we knew that the Russians were interested in dolphin studies, but not that much interested.' Rawingson looked sheepily at Keilty and Jack standing together.

'Look, Admiral . . .' Jack began, his face angry. He took a step towards Rawingson.

'Forget it, Jack.' Keilty said warily, and put a restraining hand on his shoulder. 'It's done now, and he's only one man. And if he has to depend on idiots like Redgrave and the rest of those characters, I can see some of his problems.'

Rawingson jumped up, anger beginning to show in his eyes. 'Look, you two young idiots . . .'

'I said, forget it,' Keilty interrupted sharply. 'Let's quit fighting among ourselves.' He glanced at the two Australian officers who had witnessed the enmity between the three Americans. They stood up and excused themselves hastily and left.

After they were gone, Keilty kicked the duffel bag before he spoke again. 'Admiral, Jack is upset and so am I about your acknowledged ignorance of the Soviet dolphin research. In nineteen sixty-six the Soviets made it illegal to hunt dolphins or other Cetacea in Soviet waters, except for certain kinds of whales that traditionally were taken by the whaling fleets.

They did this on the off chance that something would come of the dolphin research, most of which was being done in the U.S. by Lilly and Norris. That little item was carried by British and American newspapers. Shortly thereafter, they classified all dolphin research being done in the U.S.S.R. and you couldn't get boo out of them.

'And now you tell us,' he said quietly, 'that your office doesn't even know that they are engaged in this kind of research.'

'Wait a minute,' Rawingson yelped. 'I didn't say that. We know they are, we just do not know to what extent.'

Weston covered his face with his hands and a steady but muffled cursing filled the room. Keilty waited politely for him to stop, then inquired solicitously: 'Do you feel better now?'

'Some. But at this point, I'm damned glad I resigned my commission before I left. Hey,' he said, turning to Keilty, 'do you know what we can do with all that money now?'

'Yeah, give it to the admiral so he can hire a kindergarten class to do his intelligence work.' Laughing, he held up his hand. 'No offense, Admiral, but I would suggest you have your people do whatever it is they are supposed to do and have them check into the status of current Soviet work.'

'Admiral,' Jack put in, 'you said they could snatch somebody, wring his brains out, then put him back with phony memories. That sounds a bit far-fetched.'

Rawingson snorted. 'We're not so dumb as you two seem to think. And neither are the Reds. The technique, while fairly complicated in setup, is easy enough to use. All you need are one strait jacket, a couple of hypodermics, one full of amphetamine and the other full of some tranquillizer, an oculometer, electroencephalograph and a microvibration gauge and a galvanic skin-response recorder. Plug the electronics into a computer, hook up a tape recorder, and leave subject alone for six to eight hours. He spills his guts automatically.'

'Heh, wha . . . ?'

'Look, it's simple,' Rawingson went on patiently. 'Strap subject into specially modified strait jacket that fits from head to foot so he can't wiggle a muscle. He is completely, and I emphasize, *completely* immobile. Attach the electronics. Then feed the stimulant and depressant to him at the same time.

'Ever drink a cup of strong, black coffee, then immediately smoke a cigarette – all when you are dead tired?'

'Don't smoke,' Weston snorted.

The first part of Rawingson's answer was limited to four-letter words. 'Take my word for it, numbskull, you can feel your nerves and muscles fighting both commands from your brain. Relax . . . get set . . . relax . . . get set. Your hands will shake, your muscles twitch – actually a minor convulsion – your eyes will refuse to focus, your head will swim, and your thoughts will become jumbled.

'Of course, all this is very minor with just cigarettes and coffee, but it *is* there. Now imagine what good strong doses of a tranquillizer and pick-me-up will do, especially when you can't move a muscle. Your body has to slowly work off the effects and you damn near go crazy.

'Now, with a properly programmed computer to sort out the noise and correlate muscle and nerve signals made visible through the EEG, oculometer, microvibrations, and skin response . . .'

'What's a microvibration?' Jack inquired.

Rawingson looked at him stonily to decide whether his question was serious or not. He decided it was.

'Microvibrations are very small, almost invisible muscular movements. Hold up your hand and point your index finger,' he commanded.

Jack did so.

'Now, see the tiny movements. No matter how hard you try, you can't hold that finger perfectly still. You have a servomechanism feedback system controlling two sets of opposing muscles. One set is a tensor; the other, a flexor. A muscle can only work by tensing itself and that moves the limb one way. To go back to the original or another position, another muscle, an opposing muscle, has to pull. It's like that throughout your body. Of course the movements you see in your finger are pretty gross, but they are classified as microvibrations. In other words, every muscle in your body "vibrates". The nerve impulses that control muscles are electrical and they can be measured.

'EEG, or electroencephalograph, is a device for measuring the electrical activity generated in the brain. In a sense, these so-called electrical impulses are the by-products of thinking, because they control your body. So far, the state of the art has not progressed to the point where each minute charge of electricity can be measured, so again we are measuring relatively gross changes. In these signals are thought patterns, but on a level so low we just do not have anything sensitive enough to measure them.'

'I see,' Weston said slowly. 'What about the skin response and "ocomotor" thing?'

'Oculometer. That's a gadget for measuring eye movements.'

'Ah, the dream thing,' Weston said.

'In a way. Thought patterns are in some way related to eye movements, or probably, more properly, the other way around. The galvanic skin-response recorder measures the electrical conductivity of the skin, which changes with emotional, mental, and physical patterns.

'You see,' he said, absently taking another drink from the table, 'separately, these techniques tell us little or nothing about thought patterns. Collectively, with the proper data sorted out, they can tell us a hell of a lot.

'So what happens is that our trussed-up subject is quietly going nuts with the chemicals boiling through his system. After an hour or so, when even the most hardened thinker can no longer concentrate, carefully phrased and selected questions are asked periodically by the tape recorder. The sound is loud and rasping enough to penetrate the noise generated by his mind. No matter how hard he tries not to think of the proper answer, eventually he will. The questions are all designed on a simple yes–no basis. Each question is properly keyed from the electronics to the tape readouts and fed into the computer for correlation. After a predetermined period, everything is shut down and the subject's system is purged. Then he is thoroughly hypnotized, given a phony set of memories, and turned loose.'

'Holy gods,' Keilty exclaimed. 'You could wring a person clean in no time.'

'Exactly. When we suspect it's been done, we use the same process to find out.'

'Then how deep are the transplanted memories,' Weston asked.

'Hell, they're deep enough. After a few years they may begin to break down, but unless you really worked at it, and I mean, work with drugs and the whole show, you will never reconstruct what happened.'

'Then how can you find out it's been done? And why not hypno everybody who might become a victim?'

'Two reasons. The first is time. It takes months of treatment. Secondly, this damn process is not even bothered by hypnotic suggestion. On the contrary, it works on a subconscious level completely below hypnosis. It bypasses the conscious mind and gets right down to the basic thought process on the electrical level. Microvibration and EEG measure electrical activity in the body. The skin response measures the emotional activity and the oculometer and the microvibration are measures of eye and muscle reflex. The amphetamine and tranquillizer override the conscious and part of the subconscious mind and make it impossible to concentrate. In fact, the disappearance of concentration becomes a dead giveaway. It means that important data is coming.

'So far as we know, there is no way to beat it.'

When the admiral had finished, the three men sat quietly for some time, finishing the drinks.

'Looks like I came out of a pretty bad situation by the skin of my teeth,' Keilty commented.

'Yes, you did,' Rawingson replied seriously. 'So the next time you jokers start knocking our work, remember what I just told you. We aren't amateurs.'

'Except when it comes to knowing about the statistics of classified Soviet research on dolphins.'

Rawingson began sputtering.

He and Jack headed for the hatch, grinning at the admiral. At the hatch, Keilty turned.

'Say, Admiral, have them check into Soviet research on ESP – they classified that in sixty-three.'

'They did?' came Rawingson's startled reply, and Keilty ducked through as Rawingson jumped up and headed for the door.

On deck again, they were still laughing and breathless from the run.

'You know,' Jack chortled, 'we really shouldn't ride him like that.'

'Yeah, but you have to admit that if we don't, he'll sink back into the morass of the say-it-ain't-so types like he was when we found him. He's coming along slowly.' Keilty grinned.

CHAPTER TWELVE

Later that afternoon, Rawingson rapped on the cabin hatch.

'Come on in,' Keilty shouted.

'Can a man of little intelligence and a military background join you two sneering geniuses,' he asked as he stepped in, and sank down on an empty bunk.

Weston grinned and poured out half a glass of scotch and passed it over to him. 'Sure, Admiral.'

'Look here,' Keilty said. 'Don't take us too seriously. We aren't as smart as we pretend to be.'

Rawingson rolled his eyes up. 'Now you tell me.' He leaned back and propped a foot up on the bunk and surveyed the men across from him. Weston was stretched out on the bed, a cigarette dangling from his hand. Keilty sat resting his arms on the back of a chair. On the desk between them was a navigation map of the Riouw island chain with depths and currents marked off. A red X presumably marked the location of the sub, resting in 1100 feet of water.

Keilty sat up, and reached across to the bunk for another cigarette. He lit it, then half stood and stretched widely.

'What's up, Pete?' he asked.

Rawingson studied the drink a moment. 'Well for one thing, we'll be on location in the morning. When do you jokers plan on going after the sub, and how?'

'Funny you should ask, Admiral,' Jack muttered from beneath closed eyes, 'we were just discussing that little item.'

'I'm afraid we'll have to play it by ear for the most part,' Keilty replied. 'We'll go as soon as we can, naturally, but it's going to depend a lot on weather and how soon we can get our gear checked out. Hopefully, the day after tomorrow. According to the navigation officer, we won't reach our target area till late in the morning and we're going to need a full day of light.'

Rawingson nodded. 'Okay, that takes care of when. Now *how* do you figure to get the sub? You've been damn mysterious about that and SEATO Command, as well as Washington, London, and Canberra, want some definite answers. They're getting edgy and are on my back to find out.'

Keilty stared thoughtfully at the map for a few moments. Finally he looked up, humor crinkling his eyes. 'Well to start with, Charlie and I will go overboard and swim down to the sub. Then we'll blow it up.'

Rawingson looked pained. 'Just like that, huh? Just swim down to eleven hundred feet and boom?'

'Just like that. Swim down to eleven hundred feet.'

'And pray tell, how do you intend to accomplish this seeming miracle?'

Keilty hesitated for a long moment. 'Okay, Admiral, just to help you out. The process is for sale to the Navy and the details are proprietary. If it works and they want it, they can buy it. Otherwise, tough luck. All right?'

'All right, Dr. Keilty,' Rawingson said formally. 'No details to the Navy. Now *how*?'

Keilty stood up and turned his back to the admiral. 'Look here.'

He arched his left hand over his right shoulder until his fingers rested on a flat plastic cap. Grunting with the effort, he turned the cap and began unscrewing it. It came away to reveal a stainless-steel bayonet coupling.

'What the hell . . . ?' Rawingson jumped up from the bunk for a closer look. Protruding slightly above the skin was a round fitting containing the inner coupling. Inside the three-quarter-inch-diameter fitting he could see a pressure valve. The whole fitting was located just above the shoulder line and about three inches to the right of the spine.

'What the hell?' he repeated.

Jack had his eyes open now and was watching Rawingson's reaction with interest.

Keilty screwed the cap back on and sat down in the chair again.

'To begin with, Pete, this little gadget technically makes me a cyborg.'

'A what?' he asked weakly as he sank back down on the bunk.

'A cyborg,' Keilty repeated patiently. 'A cyborg is a partly mechanical human being. A human that has been partly mechanized would probably be a better description.

'There's nothing so outstanding about that, really. They've been around for quite a while. A guy with a hand replaced with a steel hook, if it opens and closes by muscle action, is a cyborg. A man with a mechanical leg, and so on. We've got lots of people walking around now with pacemakers to keep their hearts beating or diabetics with a pancreatic stimulator to keep their blood glucose up. They're all cyborgs. Now, they're replacing hearts with heart pumps. Last figures I saw, some four thousand people in the U.S. alone have heart pumps. All implanted in the past three years.'

'So what's that gadget got to do with you being a cyborg?' Rawingson asked. His color was beginning to return. 'I know what a cyborg is supposed to be.'

'Okay. Here's how it works. This coupling, attached to an auxiliary lung system, allows me to return quickly to the surface without wasting a couple of days in decompression. Charlie has a lung rig too, by the way. The hard part is getting back up; down is easy.'

'Come on, skip the grade-school explanations. How are you able to accomplish this feat?'

Keilty nodded to Jack, who swung his legs off the bunk and sat up. He reached out and snagged a flat metal case and pulled it over. Unsnapping the cover, he pulled out a rectangular metal container, two by three feet, and set it on the bunk next to Rawingson. Then he took a double hose connected with Y-joints and plugged one end into the machine.

Jack pointed to the other end and unscrewed a metal cap to reveal a blunt-ended, hollow needle.

'This end goes into his back,' he said quietly.

Keilty unfastened several quick-disconnect fasteners and lifted back the cover. Rawingson peered inside and saw a shiny gray bladder and several black boxes.

Keilty pointed at the bladder. 'That stuff is really a silicone membrane permeable to both oxygen and hydrogen. This is how it works. A small pump pulls sea water through the ducts up here and circulates it around the bladder. As it passes through this duct, it is compressed to make it flow faster. Heating coils along the duct bring the water temperature to ninety-eight degrees Fahrenheit. The heater is a simple isotope unit. There's a thermoelectric generator coupled to it here that produces the half watt of power to run the pump. By the time the sea water exits the duct end, it's at body temperature. The whole contraption is insulated to keep it there. The water flows around the bladder.

'This tube,' he picked up the metal flex tube, 'attaches to my back and carries blood from the superior vena cava into the silicone plastic bladder.

'The blood circulates into the bladder and passes the oxygen and hydrogen instantly into the water. The blood, minus the excess gases, then flows back through this side of the tubing into the superior vena cava and down into the heart.

'There's nothing really that complicated about it. The tubing can be bought from Dow Chemical, the pump is out of the Beckman Instruments heart pump. I just use the pump itself and throw away the rest of the gadget. The isotope heater, I bought from Westinghouse. The rest is just a matter of assembly.

'The big problem in deep dives is that the deeper you go, the greater the pressure from the water. If you are using an aqualung, the pressure control on the air supply compensates automatically and feeds you more air. In effect, it pushes more air into you so that the pressure inside your body is equal to that outside.

'Now, if you relieve that pressure too quickly, the gases in your air supply will bubble out – literally. Your bloodstream will foam and the bubbles will block arteries, capillaries, veins, and what have you. That's what's known as the bends.'

Rawingson was studying the gadget with interest. 'That's nice, but where in the world does the hydrogen come from?'

Keilty lit another cigarette. 'Our scuba gear is just a modified aqualung, but instead of compressed air, we use a mixture of oxygen and hydrogen. You know as well as I do that at depths over two hundred feet or so, the nitrogen in the air tends to come out in the bloodstream as bubbles. So you either have to spend most of your time – like eighteen to thirty-six hours – waiting at various depths to allow the nitrogen to gradually go back into solution in the blood, or else they have to keep you in a decompression chamber and readjust your internal pressure to sea level.

'Ever since Jacques Cousteau, people have been looking for a way to get down to greater depths. Cousteau's deep submergence labs and the Navy's Sealabs I, II, III, IV, and V showed that once you adjust, you can work normally. But to come back up, you have to go through a long decompression period.

'A couple of years ago, I got interested in the problem and took it to a friend of mine, a guy named Ralph Dora. He's one of the damnedest engineers you'll ever want to meet. He's a bioengineer; he understands the workings of the human body, and he's a brilliant engineer besides.

'First, he threw out all the old, mechanical ideas for getting a man up from down there and concentrated on the physiological aspects. The most important problem was the gas bubbles. Several people have tried the heavy, inert gases, like krypton, argon, neon, et cetera, but the molecules at those pressures still formed bubbles. You could get down all right and stay there, but you still had to decompress. So Ralph suggested hydrogen and it worked better than we hoped. It has the lowest molecular weight and it is just what we needed for our gadget. Mixed properly with oxygen, it worked great.'

'Come on,' Rawingson growled, 'don't hand me that. How dumb do you think I am? Any kid with a course in high-school physics will see that the hydrogen will still bubble and if you have five hundred pounds of pressure at a thousand feet, which you do, you have to have five hundred pounds of internal pressure, and that's a hell of a lot of hydrogen. It's got to go somewhere. If you come whizzing back up, you'll inflate and explode like a balloon.'

'Hell yes. Let me finish, will you.' Keilty stubbed out his cigarette and continued. 'The trick in this gadget that makes the whole thing work is the bladder. As you say, at a thousand feet, you have five hundred pounds of pressure inside you, all of it oxygen and hydrogen gas. You have to get rid of it and fast. Now, where is that gas. What part of the body?'

'The bloodstream of course . . . hey, wait . . .' The light suddenly dawned on Rawingson.

'Right. As you start your ascent, the blood, filled with gases, circulates into the bladder and the oxygen and hydrogen diffuse through the bladder wall because of the slight pressure differential created by the sea water. As you rise, the pressure lessens and so does the volume of gas in your blood, because it's escaping through the bladder. By the time you reach the surface, the two-gas regulator has cut over to pure oxygen and the hydrogen is completely flushed out. No gas bubbles, no embolisms. Simple, what?'

'I'll be damned,' Rawingson ejaculated.

'Yeah, and you probably are too,' Weston retorted. 'It works. Mort and Charlie both have made several dives to eight hundred feet and back with no ill effects.'

'This crazy thing works on the porp . . . dolphin too?'

'Sure, why not? Same physiological setup – with a few differences of course – but not enough to interfere. We have limited our stay time at great depths to five minutes so far, because we still don't know what effect the high pressure will have on the body's chemical reactions. But it works and we can reach the sub!'

'Well, how come if you had this rig, you didn't use it with Charlie on the first dive?'

'Two reasons. First of all, a dolphin on sonar looks a lot like a man unless he comes up to breathe every few minutes. They might have mistaken him for a shark, but I doubt it. They probably used shark repellent around the tower, both for safety and for security reasons.

'Secondly, this gadget works best below two hundred feet where there is enough pressure to make its use worthwhile. Until that depth, you might as well use regular scuba gear and compressed air.'

'Then that thing on your shoulder is attached to the vein in your back?' Rawingson asked.

'Yep. It's sewn into the vein walls. The superior vena cava runs down the thorax and directly into the heart. It's the largest and closest attachment point in the back that can be used for the "lung" hookup.'

Rawingson was now sitting on the edge of the bunk with his head and shoulders hunched in concentration over the opened 'lung'. Keilty's head was next to his as he traced out the flow pattern through the system. Weston, lying on the bunk and observing them, was struck by the paradox in the scene. He would have sworn two weeks earlier that Keilty would never again have had anything to do with the Navy, the military in general, or the U.S. Government, yet here they were, heads together, deeply involved in a technical discussion.

He rolled back and shut his eyes. He was bushed, and besides, his shoulder ached. Weston grinned to himself. Keilty still had not seen the third 'lung'! When he did, there would be hell to pay. Grinning widely, he fell asleep.

Rawingson and Keilty talked on for another hour until Rawingson sat up and stopped in the middle of a sentence.

'What's the matter?' Keilty asked.

Rawingson stood up and leaned across the bunk to look out the opened porthole.

'Sea's roughing up a bit. We're going to be in for some weather tonight.'

'Monsoon finally going to hit, hey?' Keilty rubbed his hands in anticipation. 'I always wanted to ride a big boat during a good blow.'

'Hmm, you may get your chance tonight.' He stared out a moment longer, then sat down again on the bunk. 'Don't forget, if the monsoon does hit, it could foul up the operation pretty badly.'

'It could at that,' Keilty admitted. 'You know, this is the first time I've been in this part of the world. What's a monsoon like?'

Rawingson thought for a moment. 'The initial storm is pretty much like the hurricanes you get down in the Keys, some years. The barometer drops steadily for a couple of days, then all of a sudden you find yourself in the middle of a force nine gale. Winds up to eighty or ninety knots, the rain smashing in level sheets like someone is hitting you with a fire hose. The waves will rise to twenty feet or better with the crests being blown right off ahead of the wind.

'The rain and winds will keep up for eight to ten hours, then drop away to five to ten knots. The waves will die to pretty solid breakers at ten feet or less. It's particularly bad in this part of the South China Sea due to the currents and cross-currents caused by the islands and the strait. After the initial blow, the winds only come with the rains, then only at twenty to thirty knots.

'It's funny, a lot of people think of the monsoon as six months of continual rain. Actually that isn't so. It only rains a couple of hours just after noon, but when it does, it comes down in buckets, up to an inch of rain in one hour.

'Getting back to the "lung" system,' Rawingson said, 'it works the same way for Charlie?'

'Yes,' said Keilty. 'It works pretty much the same way. Remember earlier I told you that a dolphin has a lung relatively the same size as a man's. Well, the general arrangement of his anatomy is somewhat similar. In the dolphin, the superior vena cava runs across where his right shoulder is. You know his flippers are actually atrophied legs. Originally he was a sea animal that took a crack at the land and developed legs, et cetera, probably even walked erect towards the end, or almost so. Then he decided he didn't like the land. Maybe too much competition. That was roughly near the end of the Reptile Age and he went back to the sea, and by now he's almost completely reverted.

'I've thought many times,' Keilty continued slowly, 'that perhaps we're reaching the end of our string as complete masters of the planet. Could be that the dolphin will challenge us, at least as far as the oceans go. They're as intelligent as hell, as much or more so than man, if Charlie's any indication.

But it's such a long, slow process trying to pump him for information, because at each step we have to establish a mutual communication basis for each new concept. You would never realize how many individual concepts we juggle every day and don't even think about.

'But I wish we could learn more about his early life. I think that's a key, maybe even *the* key. But because he still has only a hazy conception of time and yesterday means little or nothing to him, I get the feeling that I am continually underestimating him and it's damned frustrating.'

He paused and shook his head. 'Anyway, that's another problem; to answer your question – yes, it does work the same way. Instead of an implanted bayonet valve, we just insert a large-diameter hypodermic needle into the vein with a local anesthetic.'

'And that's all it takes?'

'Sure. Because the essential thing is to circulate the gas-laden blood into the bladder and there's not as much blood in a dolphin to scrub the wastes from. They have a wonderful survival mechanism, as you would expect of an air-breathing mammal living in the sea. They only circulate enough blood to keep their body working and the rest is shunted into storage tanks. That's why, although they're relatively the same size, they can stay down longer than humans. They have to aerate only the blood needed to keep them going.'

Rawingson sat for some moments thinking, before shifting his position.

'You're sure it works?'

'Like Jack says, I tried it several times. With Charlie along, I got down to eight hundred feet.'

'For how long?' Rawingson asked suspiciously.

'Well, ah . . . for long enough to know that it works.'

'But not for ten minutes, or a half hour?'

'Look,' Keilty growled, 'what the hell difference does it make? We're going. You got any better ideas on how to pull it off?'

'Well no . . .' Rawingson started.

'Well no is right. So shut up. We've made some improvements since the last test and they'll work all right. The last thing in the world that sub will expect is an attack by individuals. So that's how we do it.'

Rawingson regarded him stonily for several moments. Finally he slapped his hands on his knees and stood up.

'All right, you bastard. Go get killed. Your patriotism is admirable, though somewhat short-sighted. However, you are the only one we have that is anywhere near capable of doing the job.'

'Patriotism,' Keilty snorted. 'I spell that d-o-l-l-a-r-s.'

Rawingson paused at the hatchway and uttered one short, four-letter expletive. 'Don't try and kid granddad, sonny,' and went out chuckling.

Keilty stared at the closed hatch for quite a while, then stretched out on the vacated bunk, kicked his sneakers off, and promptly fell asleep.

CHAPTER THIRTEEN

Keilty awoke early and completely and braced himself against the rolling of the cruiser, folded both hands behind his head, and turned to reviewing his nebulous plans for finding the Chinese sub. The seas were roughing up again as the monsoon season progressed with no monsoon. The cruiser was wallowing heavily in the climbing waves, but the rain had still not broken in appreciable amounts.

He had spent the previous day with Charlie and Jack, checking equipment and fitting and adjusting the harnesses they would wear. Charlie had seemed preoccupied, but kept assuring him that he was perfectly all right and ready to go at any time.

He rolled over on his side and looked over to Jack's blanketed form wedged diagonally in the bunk. Since Jack was still asleep, he got out of bed, took a quick shower, quietly shaved and dressed, and left.

The full force of the cold wind struck him as he stepped through the hatch and spatters of rain struck fitfully on the deck and upperworks. Keeping close to the metal walls, he moved along the bucking deck aft towards the mess.

The mess was warm and cheerful and almost empty. Keilty filled a tray with eggs and ham, drew a mug of hot, black tea and moved off to a table alone to think. Over more tea and a first cigarette, he let his thoughts dwell on the coming day. There had been a minor change in plans. They would be coming on station by midafternoon. The drill was that he and Charlie would make a scouting dive, both to check their equipment and to let the dolphin re-establish the location of the sub – if it was still there. That would give him the morning to finish going over the equipment with Charlie and let them both catch a two-hour nap. Then, tomorrow morning, just as soon as it was light enough for a helicopter to get them in, they would go after the sub.

His thoughts were interrupted by the approach of a burly chief petty officer. Keilty glanced up to see a red-faced Australian topping better than six and a half feet. He wore an immaculate chef's white hat and a tee-shirt with an insignia sewn on the chest.

'Tha coptain passed the wurd, you've a dorty mission cumming op,' he announced in a Scots brogue so thick that Keilty could barely understand him.

'Mon like ye needs all tha fuel he con eat. De ye won more?'

Keilty leaned back and grinned. 'Sure do. Those were the best eggs I've had since I left home. But, like you say, six are hardly filling. How about another order?'

The cook nodded ponderously, then his face exploded into a deep grin that drew his mouth up and his eyebrows down until his face almost completed a full circle.

'Onnytime yer aboard, Dockter.' Still grinning, he went back to the galley where muffled Celtic cursing erupted.

Keilty sat musing over the rest of the tea until a rating brought him a second round of breakfast. Halfway through, he saw Weston stumble through the hatchway and peer around. Keilty waved him over to his table and he collapsed onto the bench with a groan and made a sincere attempt to prop his eyelids open with his fingers. The rating came back.

'Your order, sir?'

Jack groaned again and buried his head in his arms.

'Low blood sugar,' Keilty explained. 'Bring him the same thing, and coffee – black – right away.'

When he was gone, Jack looked up slowly without lifting his head.

'I'll be damned,' Keilty said. 'How you ever lasted as long as you did in the Coast Guard is a mystery to me. I've never seen anybody so slow to wake up in the morning.'

'Aw shut up.'

Keilty chuckled. 'Waking up is a slow process, but relentless, nevertheless. At least now you are able to put some feeling into it. Five minutes ago, you couldn't have done that.'

'Five minutes ago, I was still sleeping.'

'So, what woke you up? I figured you were good for another hour or two yet.'

Weston groaned. 'Fell out. This damn boat's jumping around like a cork. Sunny tropics.' The rest of the dissertation was delivered in expletives, some of which Keilty had not heard before.

'Always did admire a man with a good grasp of profanity. Now drink your coffee so I can talk to you.'

Weston took the cup from the rating and sipped cautiously, then drained the cup. He caught the steward as he passed the table and made him leave a pot.

'Good. Now at least, your eyes are open. After you flaked

out on us yesterday . . .' He held up a restraining hand. '. . . we got a briefing from Intelligence. And it ain't so good, as the man said.'

'So let's have it – in ten words or less.'

'Briefly, signs of activity have increased along the Red Chinese border in the Kazakhstan-Singkiang area or on the Manchurian border. Kind of looks like we may have joggled the Russians' elbow with that business the other night and they decided to move faster. Also, there are indications that elements of the Vietnamese navy may be assembling off Java Head. There were several incidents along the Cambodian border last night as well. Also, signs of other activity along the Mekong. So what it boils down to is that we've been requested . . .' he emphasized the word sarcastically . . . 'to move and move fast.'

'When?' Weston was thoroughly awake now.

'This afternoon. We go on a scouting mission. Tomorrow morning, early, we hit them.'

Weston sat up a little straighter. 'What the hell do they mean by "signs of activity have increased"?'

Keilty shrugged. 'Probably the same old routine. One of the surveillance satellites probably picked up some coolie lighting a cigarette on his way home last night and it sent everybody into a tizzy.'

Weston snorted and shoveled his mouth full.

'But,' Keilty continued, 'it's probably a good idea to move fast; just in case there are any leaks.'

'Yeah,' Weston mumbled. 'Damn, it's too early in the morning for me to think deep thoughts. When did you say we go get the sub?'

'Tomorrow morning.'

'Tomorrow morning! Ye gods, you don't even give me time to work the kinks out.'

'Kinks, what for?'

Weston sat back, surprise on his face. 'What for? You think I'm gonna let you go charging off with that crazy fish – both of you alone? If you do, you're nuts.'

'Wait, boy, back off a minute. What are you talking about?' Keilty's puzzlement wasn't as deep as he made out, but he did not like what Jack was leading up to. 'You weren't thinking you were going along, were you?'

'You're darn right. You're not thinking I was going to let

you two go off alone, were you?' he countered. 'Come on, admit it, I'm twice the diver you'll ever be. You go after that sub, you'll never come back. And you'll get Charlie killed in the process.'

Keilty shook his head, then faced Weston. 'Let's get one thing straight, friend. I'm going, and that's that. So how you gonna stop me, break my arm?'

A light gleamed deep in Weston's eyes. 'I hadn't considered that, but it's not a bad idea.' He started to rise.

Keilty looked at his face and saw that he was dead serious.

'Hey now, wait a minute. They hired *me*. And they paid *me*. Not you.'

'The only indispensable man on this team is Charlie. Not you,' Weston answered angrily. 'You're a good diver all right, but not that good. Look, from what Charlie says, that sub is resting in close to eleven hundred feet of water. Even with the "lung" you couldn't take that depth. Not for ten minutes anyway. For God's sake, Charlie's limit is only twenty minutes at eight hundred feet, and he's built for that kind of work, at least more so than you.'

'And you!'

'Okay, so I haven't been to a thousand feet with a "lung" either, but the fact still stands, neither have you.'

'Damn it, you aren't going,' Keilty said stubbornly. 'It's too dangerous.'

'Yeah, suicide. And you're walking right into it. With three, the chances are a hundred per cent better.'

The two men faced each other across the table, their expressions set in anger at the other's stubbornness.

'I'll make it.'

'Like hell you will.' Weston slammed the mug down and attacked the eggs furiously.

After several minutes, Keilty muttered.

'What?'

'I said,' he shouted, 'do you want to come along and hold my hand?'

Jack's head shot up. 'Yeah,' he shouted back around a mouthful.

The men looked at each other and burst into laughter.

'You . . . you . . .' Keilty choked, 'that's what you wanted all along, you bastard. Ever since you stepped on that plane. That's why you resigned.'

Weston laughed harder than ever.

'Now what?' Keilty chortled.

'I never eat breakfast.' Weston collapsed, holding his sides, and roared.

CHAPTER FOURTEEN

The monsoon, previewed by several weeks of light squalls mixed with humid and oppressive moments of quietude, finally blazed out of the stewpot of the southwest Pacific, lashing the coasts of Australia before sweeping northwesterly across the fabled seas of the Orient. H.M.A.S. *Vigilant*, caught in the northern reaches of the Java Sea, buried her bows in the smoking waves and dug in. Her roll became more pronounced as she struck out crosswise under full power into the towering seas. Wave crests topped twenty-five feet as she plowed towards the Riouw Archipelago, less than four hours away.

The meteorologist clambered forward, hanging onto the hastily rigged emergency lines, the waterproof packet containing the latest meteorological reports jammed into his blouse beneath a streaming slicker. He stomped into the warm, dimly lit wheelhouse and formed a puddle on the floor while he struggled out of the slicker.

The captain waved him over to where he was standing in front of the revolving screen and read the report, while the met. officer sipped a mug of hot tea. Outside, the sun was a brighter spot in the leaden gray sky, all but obscured by the driving rain and the waves, which were often higher than the mast when she bellied into a trough. Wisps of foam streamed forward ahead of the advancing waves, driven by the stiffening wind. Curiously enough, the sky was grayish but the seas were coppery, shading to pale gold near the crests.

The barometer had been falling steadily since the evening before, while the wind increased in fitful gusts.

'Force five?' the captain asked.

'Yessir, but both wind and rain could stop for a short while this afternoon . . . about fourteen hundred hours, I should think.'

He paused to study the report once more.

'Captain's compliments to the admiral, and will he see me immediately?'

As a rating left to deliver the message, the captain turned back to the met. officer. 'Thank you, Lieutenant Higgins. Please keep me informed of any changes.'

Five minutes later, he was having coffee with Admiral Collins and explaining the worsening weather.

'So there is no hope that the gale will lighten enough to-morrow to get them in?'

'No, sir. The seas are much too high. The met. reports indicate that wind and rain may lessen enough to launch a helicopter by midafternoon.'

The admiral sipped at his coffee thoughtfully. 'Perhaps we should get Dr. Keilty up here and find out what his plans are.'

Keilty rapped quickly on the hatch and pushed in. 'Good morning, Admiral, Captain.'

Both men replied, and the admiral offered him coffee and a chair. 'Our latest met. reports indicate worsening wave conditions through this evening with a full gale for the next two days, as you may have guessed. However, the wind and rain both are due to slack off about noon for a few hours, hopefully enough to launch a helicopter.'

'Ah . . . we had planned on making this afternoon's run a scouting mission, more of a shakedown cruise than anything else. But we could get along without it and go on schedule tomorrow morning.' Keilty sipped at the hot coffee.

The admiral looked uncomfortable. Before he could reply, a striker stuck his head into the cabin and announced Admiral Rawingson.

He strode briskly into the cabin, his face set and grim. 'Gentlemen, we must move now, immediately,' he began without preliminaries. 'I've just received this message from Washington.' He waved a yellow flimsy. 'The Vietnamese and Cambodian armies have moved hard against the Malaysian border. They think it's not a diversion but the beginning of the real thing. Russian maneuvers are picking up again on the Manchurian border, probably as a warning to the Chinese to mind their own business. NORAD also reports Soviet Air and Rocket Forces on first stage yellow alert.'

Keilty slammed his fist down onto the chair arm. 'What about the sub?'

'We don't know yet. But you can bet it won't stay idle long.'

'Admiral,' Keilty turned to both Australian officers, 'how close can we get to the sub before it spots us?'

They exchanged glances. 'About thirty miles, I would think,' Captain Whittlson replied slowly.

'How long before we get to within thirty miles?'

'Three hours and forty minutes at flank speed.'

'Okay, it's nearly ten o'clock now. By one-forty we should be on station. What does your weather report say about winds in that area?'

'Winds should be twenty-five knots, but still raining.'

'All right. Have you got a good helicopter pilot?'

'Hey wait,' Rawingson exploded, 'you can't get a helicopter off this ship in twenty-foot waves and twenty-five knots of wind.'

'Want to bet? Look, I'm not going to stand here arguing. Thirty miles is too far to swim. A helicopter can put us down almost directly over the sub – if it's still there. But if you fiddle around waiting for good weather, you could be here a week and the sub won't. It couldn't care less what the surface conditions are. If your intelligence reports are right, that sub has four nuclear guided missiles. It might not even have to surface to fire them. If the Reds moved this morning, three days ahead of schedule, they suspect the Allies are on to them and they want the first jump. And you had better start praying that the sub is still there, 'cause if it isn't, you won't find it again until it's too late. And they won't be gentlemen about it either and just try and blow up the strait. There are at least six capitals within a two-thousand-mile striking range. Lose them, plus Singapore and the straits fleet, and you've lost the war.'

Keilty jammed a cigarette in his mouth and continued pacing.

Rawingson said, 'I'm afraid he's right again, gentlemen. The fact that we've heard nothing from the Vietnamese and have no information that shows military moves beyond assembly points makes me think that they know what's coming. Their main interest is Singapore. They failed the first time and now they have an enlarged Allied fleet, three times as powerful, to contend with. If Singapore is destroyed, they lose their reason for war. I think at this point they will wait until they see how successful the Soviets are before they commit themselves. Right now the Chinese may be in deep trouble. We have word from Peking and have a tentative approach for Allied operations.' He paused and looked at the three men.

'It's beginning to look as if we can catch the Vietnamese in the pincers, instead of the other way around. They know, but don't know that we know – I hope – that everything will hinge on that sub.'

'You're damn right it will,' Keilty yelled, 'so instead of act-ing like a debating society, let's get cracking.' He went out the hatch, earlier misgivings forgotten, while the captain was calling the bridge to order flank speed.

Below in the medical quarters, he described the new turn of events to Jack and Charlie. Weston immediately began checking equipment, his eyes gleaming with excitement. Charlie, on the other hand, sank back into the tank until only his chin was resting on the padded edge.

Keilty noticed the troubled expression and planted himself in front of the dolphin.

'So now what's eating you? I thought you said a couple of days ago you wanted to see some action to relieve your boredom.'

'True, I did say that,' Charlie said slowly into the microphone. He had been thinking that now he was about to commit himself to a course of action that he had hoped to avoid. But Keilty was his friend and he had promised. Human affairs were about to become his affairs for good.

'This is *no* time for philosophy,' he muttered. Then louder, 'I suppose I have to wear that damned pack again.'

Keilty, taken aback, laughed. 'Yes, you do, but Jack's brought a wet suit for you, so it shouldn't chafe your tender side.'

Charlie muttered a heartfelt 'Good!'

The three donned special plastic suits supplied with pure oxygen to purge nitrogen and other gases from their system that could embolize on the fast ascent. They spent the next two hours checking out the equipment, with special attention to the two communication devices. The first was an emergency communicator, looking quite a bit like a Very pistol, but instead of a flare, the gun was designed to launch from underwater a rocket which contained a high-speed tape recorder in its nose. The rocket was propelled by compressed air to the surface, where a solid fuel charge ignited and carried the recorder to two thousand feet. At the high point of its trajectory, the recorder was triggered and it transmitted forty seconds of taped information in one millisecond for a radius of sixty miles. An omnidirectional antenna was built into the casing of the rocket.

The second communication device was for continual transmission. They were sure that the submarine crew would be jumpy enough continuously to monitor for stray radio signals, yet the command ship had to have some means of keeping a directional beam on the three of them. They were, in effect, a dead man's switch; as long as they transmitted every twenty seconds, the ship would know they were still functioning. If the signal ceased, then the cruiser would have to move in with depth charges and subrocs in the hope that they would still have time to find and destroy the sub.

For their device, they had turned to the Australian Navy Research Branch, which had come up with a simple battery-driven clicker. The frequency and amplitude of the clicks it produced were the same as those made by mollusks, which abounded in the area. When one mollusk clicked, it acted as an exciting signal and every other mollusk within hearing distance also clicked once.

On the completion of the mission and when the three had surfaced, a specially designed sonarbuoy attached to Jack's harness would be released. It would sink to the fifty-foot level and begin transmitting a sonar signal audible for better than fifty nautical miles. Its batteries would last fourteen hours. With the Very pistol, the sonarbuoy, and the *Vigilant*'s own radar and sonar, they should be easily picked up.

As Keilty, Weston, and Charlie moved in towards the sub, the clicker mounted on Charlie's back pack would click every twenty seconds, and the mollusks would also click. The clicker was mounted on Charlie's pack and keyed to his breathing. If he stopped breathing, the ship would be warned. A simple enough device, but never actually tested in the open sea. All they could do was hope. They had chosen Charlie to carry the device because he was the most important member of the three-man team. In addition, each would carry two specially designed bombs, weighing ten pounds apiece.

Weston picked one up and fingered the deflated air cell attached to the handle. 'Who thought this little beauty up?'

'They tell me that's another new piece of equipment their special branch came up with. It has a shaped charge of amatol that can punch an armor-piercing cartridge through a foot of high-carbon steel. There is also a second, slower explosive which will set up oscillation waves along the hull. The six bombs will set up interfering waves and literally shake the sub to pieces. There's a one-hundred-and-twenty-second timer on each bomb. A couple of these should be enough to breach the sub's hull. Water pressure will do the rest. At least that's the theory,' Keilty grinned.

'I suppose it's never been tested either.'

'Nope.'

They spent the rest of the hour checking and stowing the last pieces of gear. Then Keilty left Weston to supervise the crew rigging Charlie's tank for the helicopter, while he went forward to the bridge for a last briefing. He found Rawingson, Admiral Collins, and the captain waiting for him at the chart table with the pilot of the helicopter. He was introduced to Lieutenant Atkins, a gangling, yet sturdy Queenslander with a thatch of carefully combed blond hair.

'So how's the weather look?' Keilty asked, peering at the driving rain through the revolving screen. The waves seemed to have moderated slightly and were no longer making the *Vigilant* heel sharply as they broke over the bow.

'The wind is dying and the end of the rain squall is in sight,' Rawingson said with worry overlaying the tones of confidence in his voice. 'Lieutenant Atkins thinks he should have no real trouble.'

Keilty turned to Atkins. The pilot had an easy smile on his face and gave Keilty a wink of confidence.

'It'll be a matter of picking the right wave, sir,' he said in broad Australian accents. 'Once in the air, it'll be rough, but we should do all right. With the new inertial compass, we shouldn't have any trouble finding the right spot. Perhaps I'll be able to set you down right over the sub.'

'Good,' Keilty replied. 'I'll leave that end up to you. But don't forget, there's only one good long-distance swimmer in the three of us.'

'Don't worry too much about that. I'll try and hang over the spot long enough to direct one of the MTBs in when I see the sub go.'

For the next ten minutes, the four men went over the operation completely. The copter would set them down half a mile or so from the sub. They would depend on Charlie's sonar capability to home them in. Each would take one part of the sub: Weston, the bow; Keilty, midship; and Charlie, the stern. Each would mount his two bombs twenty feet apart, one on the deck, the other on the hull above the ballast tanks. All six mines would be set for the full 120 seconds. The mines contained a powerful battery-powered electromagnet, and so would make no sound as they were attached. After all the mines were set, they would backtrack as fast as possible until they went off. Hopefully, the concussion would do no more than shake them up. Charlie would then round up the two humans, and they would surface and release smoke flares and the radio sonarbuoy to aid the MTB in picking them up.

The met. crew estimated four-foot waves in the vicinity of the islands. They were to be about three miles offshore and had no worries about reefs.

Satisfied that everything was planned as closely as possible, Keilty left to pick up his gear. When he came on deck again, hauling his heavy 'lung' pack after him, he could feel the ship turning to run with the waves. The lurching and heeling had leveled out somewhat as the ship settled firmly on its new course.

Atkins was already idling the blades of the big Avro Roe copter. Rawingson stepped forward for a last 'good luck' and a firm handshake.

'Hey, Pete, ever consider leaving the Navy?' Keilty shouted over the wind and noise of the gas-turbine engine. 'Got a good spot on the team open for you.'

Rawingson grinned and pushed him forward. Keilty clambered up the ladder, assisted by two crewmen, who slung his pack aboard. Keilty edged around Charlie's tank and stowed his pack in a locker behind the copilot's seat, then checked Charlie over.

The dolphin's tank had been drained and he was resting on oil-filled cushions, looking completely unhappy and alien in the plastic suit and fitted packs. The metal pack containing the 'lung' was strapped just behind his dorsal fin with the two jointed hoses leading to the hypodermic connector which Weston would insert before they left the copter. The two humans would hook each other up in the water.

Weston, snugging down the last safety belt, gave Keilty a thumbs-up signal and strapped himself down.

Keilty climbed forward into the copilot's seat.

'You chaps all set?' Atkins asked. Through the windshield and the wipers, Keilty could see most of the off-watch crew clustered around the helicopter pad on the rain- and spray-slick deck. The looming mass of the superstructure was straight ahead. They were angled off to the starboard side of the cruiser to give the pilot clear visibility past the bow so he could judge the height of the waves.

'We'll wait until the ruddy boat tops a crest. We have to be well on our way before she rises again,' Atkins informed Keilty.

Keilty nodded. Ahead, he could see one of the MTBs on station several hundred yards in front of the larger ship. She would attempt to pick them up if they went in, but there certainly would not be much chance of getting out of the chopper's cramped cabin.

The MTB disappeared as she dropped into a trough. Atkins ran the turbine up to full-rated power and rested his hand on the black pitch control. At the moment the blades carried no pitch, and consequently, very little lift. He signaled for the winches that held her down to free, and the cables fell away and snaked across the deck. The cruiser cleared a wave, hung poised for the barest of instants, then dropped.

Atkins twisted the pitch knob and yanked the column back. Keilty felt the helicopter lurch and heard the landing gear squeal as they touched down hard. Then they were in the air. Atkins face was grim as he hauled back, one hand tending the throttle. A gust of wind caught them and he slipped power, then full on again to miss an arm of the radar antenna.

The deck became a glistening trough in the wild waves, and then they were in the overcast fighting for altitude. The winds caught at the fragile copter, slamming it from side to side, shaking it like a terrier. Sweat stood out on Atkins' face and gleamed dully in the gray twilight as he fought for control with the elements. At two thousand feet, he leveled off and cut the power and pitch back. As the copter came around with the wind, the buffeting slackened off.

'Pretty rough, I'd say,' Atkins muttered tightly. Keilty missed the words but not the meaning.

They checked to see that Weston and Charlie were still with them. Both were slightly airsick and bruised from the shaking, but otherwise okay.

Atkins warmed up the inertial compass and fed co-ordinates to it.

'Okay, back there, hold on. The next half an hour is going to be rough,' and he swung the helicopter back into the cross wind.

The next half hour *was* rough. The copter bored on across the wind. Streamers of rain slashed briefly against the windshield as the wind veered suddenly. They flew on for what seemed like forever to Keilty. The gray fog pressed in against the windshield, and with the noise of the engine and the shaking and vibration of the wind, only the flight programmer gave any indication that they were moving. Keilty was sweating heavily inside the suit, and the pure oxygen had given him a raging headache. Atkins' face was tense with strain as he stared at the instruments, his hands and feet never still as he rode the rudder and altitude controls.

To Charlie, it was a nightmare of shaking on the unfamiliar oil cushions. The skin beneath his plastic suit drew tighter as it dried, until he felt ready to crawl out of the tank and cursed himself for his part in this suicidal undertaking.

After thirty-five minutes, Atkins began losing altitude until they broke from beneath the cloud cover. The seas looked the same to Keilty, except for the absence of the cruiser and MTBs. Ahead was a barely discernible smudge on the horizon that marked Atuk Island. As they dropped lower towards the waves, the wind lessened until Keilty estimated that it was blowing less than twenty knots.

The pilot swung the copter into a shallow circle, dropping lower all the time, until he was barely ten feet above the waves.

'This should be it,' he shouted to Keilty. 'You'll have to jump for it from here.'

'What about you?' Keilty shouted back. 'You can't hold in this wind.'

'I know. I'll have to go back. If we don't hear from you, I'll give you thirty minutes from the time you go in, and then radio the *Vigilant* to move in.'

Keilty nodded, gripped the man's shoulder in thanks, and pulled himself back to the tank. Weston was already unstrapped and wrestling the tank to the door. Between them, they got it centered and ready to go. Keilty worked the straps loose and climbed into the tank with the dolphin. Weston pushed him aside and unfastened the small case that contained the connector hypodermic. He checked to see that the tank contained enough local anaesthetic to last for an hour. Then he swabbed the marked area on Charlie's broad back with alcohol. Charlie rolled his eyes up towards Keilty, who grinned and patted his head.

'Take it easy, old friend.'

Jack hesitated a moment, then inserted the needle just as Charlie gave his characteristic cough that indicated he was breathing in. Keilty grabbed the coaming as Jack upended the tank and Charlie slid out in a steep dive, free of the copter.

The tank settled again and Keilty climbed to the edge and peered out. The blades of the helicopter beating against the fine rain sprayed his face with mist. He knuckled his eyes free of water and saw Charlie reappear below, his curiously humped back breaking the surface momentarily; then he submerged again.

Keilty glanced around. Weston was at his arm.

'Next,' he yelled cheerfully over the noise. Keilty nodded and checked to make sure his back pack was secure and that his face mask was safely tucked inside the blouse of his wet suit and jumped. Rain spattered his face briefly; then he hit the water headfirst, hands pointed over his head. The bone-chilling cold of the supposedly warm water shocked him and he surfaced gasping.

The copter was no longer directly above him, but Atkins was beating back against the wind. As the copter drifted back over him, Weston dove out, lower than Keilty, and hit the water fifty yards from him. In a moment, his head reappeared and he waved at the copter. Charlie surfaced alongside of Keilty and emitted a muffled squeak. Keilty waved to Atkins to indicate that everything was all right, and the helicopter gained altitude until it was lost in the low-hanging clouds again.

The rain was falling lightly now and shortly Jack reached them.

'All present and accounted for, I see,' he shouted cheerfully, over the wind.

The two men went over the drill again and checked Charlie's equipment when he surfaced. They stripped out of the plastic coveralls and clamped their masks on quickly.

'Turn around. You first.' Keilty still had to yell to make himself heard. The noise of the copter hovering overhead drowned out everything else.

'You sure you'll be okay?'

Weston nodded and lifted his back out of the water until he was resting on an inflated air pillow.

'When I hook you up, go under for a few minutes to make sure it's working properly, then come up and fix mine.'

Weston nodded. Keilty moved over to him and opened the connector flap. They had hooked themselves up earlier in the morning to check out the systems. Keilty pulled the hose out of its container and wiped the bayonet end with his hand, then inserted it and gave it a half turn, locking the connection securely. He gave Jack a tap on the 'lung' cover and watched him submerge.

The copter still hung above them, creating a flattened and rippled area where its downdraught blew the waves flat. He could imagine the strain as Atkins fought to hang over them in the strong wind.

Weston surfaced again alongside him and he was ready, lying on the air pillow. He felt Jack's strong hands as he worked quickly to open the plastic cap and make the connection. When he felt Jack's tap, he slipped beneath the waves. Charlie and Jack appeared simultaneously alongside him, and Jack pressed the life line into his hand.

CHAPTER FIFTEEN

Keilty was first on the twenty-foot line attached to Charlie's harness. He clipped his ear-plug lead onto the life line.

'. . . is about half a mile ahead. Pretty fancy flying,' Charlie was saying.

Keilty felt a tug on the line and began swimming forward. He glanced over his shoulder to see the dim figure of Weston gliding silently behind.

Half a mile. He hoped that silly clicker on Charlie's pack was working. It was going to take them a while to reach that sub. Charlie started swimming down quickly. After five minutes, he found himself tiring from the heavy burden of the pack he was carrying. Then he cursed himself for an ass. He had forgotten to fill the water sacs.

The dim light filtering down from the violently rippling surface was quickly left behind. Even at the start, Keilty could hardly see more than the powerful tail flukes ahead of him moving up and down tirelessly, and soon he found himself surrounded by complete blackness. Already, his leg muscles were beginning to tire and he realized how much out of shape he was. The bulky projections of the equipment and mines attached to his belt and back made swimming that much harder. He thought of checking with both Jack and Charlie to see how they were doing, then decided not to. No sense in admitting so early that Jack may have had a point.

He pushed doggedly on for another five minutes before calling a halt. Charlie looped back as Weston moved up. Keilty unslung the pistol and an oversized cartridge.

'Everyone okay?' he asked. Both Charlie's and Weston's acknowledgment came back quickly. Charlie's voice, coming both through the transphonemator and the underwater voice membrane, assumed almost its normal squeal-like pitch, while Jack's was low and distorted.

'How far to go, Charlie?' he asked.

'We're getting closer now. From here, we go straight down. We have little more than a quarter of a mile left. I am sure it is a submarine. Nothing else seems to be moving and it looks like it's in the same place that it was when I saw it last.'

'Okay, group. Soon as I send off this report, we go and get

it.' He clipped the cartridge to the neckband microphone and dictated the information tersely. Then he opened the breech of the pistol and inserted the cartridge. With the muzzle above his head and pointed to the surface, he pulled the trigger. There was a soft whoosh, and the pistol jerked very gently in his hand. Looking up, all he could see was a rising stream of CO_2 bubbles. He spread his hands in resignation and they took up the trek again.

They dove deeper and deeper until the only light was the dim luminous twin dial of the depth gauge and chronometer on his wrist. The figures of both Charlie and Jack had long since been lost in the black murk and the only sensations left to him were the occasional sounds of breathing in his ear plug and the steady tug on the line.

Suddenly he became aware of the absence of a second sound that should have blanked everything else out. Charlie's clicker was working away steadily, but there were no answering sounds from the ocean floor, now less than thirty feet beneath them. The research boys had told him that he should be able to hear the mollusks as soon as they reached the nine-hundred-foot level. At the same time, the tug on the line slackened and he felt Charlie's tail flukes graze his cheek.

'What's the matter?' Jack asked.

'Listen,' Keilty commanded. 'There's no noise from those damn mollusks.'

There was a short silence, punctuated only with the sound of breathing.

'So there isn't,' Jack replied slowly.

Keilty felt Charlie's rough hide scrape against his arm.

'That isn't all – the submarine is moving,' Charlie said.

Keilty muttered a four-letter expletive to himself. 'What about the cruiser?'

There was a short silence from Charlie; then, 'I can't tell, it's out of my range probably.'

Keilty pulled the pistol from his belt and clipped the cartridge to the neckband microphone again and for several seconds recorded a message. Then he inserted the cartridge into the Very pistol and fired it towards the surface.

'Let's hope it's not too late,' muttered Keilty. 'I warned them to stay away.'

'You didn't tell them the sub was moving, did you?' said Weston.

'Not on your life. They find that out and all hell's gonna break loose. Before they could find and destroy it, she will have fired all her missiles.'

Keilty was surprised at how sluggish he felt. The cold water had thoroughly numbed him and every time he moved, he felt as if he were trying to swim in heavy molasses. A series of pains had begun across his chest and succeeding breaths were causing him to gasp. They were almost nine hundred feet down now, and they were blind, except for Charlie's sonar vision. The miniature instrument readouts lining his mask rim were all into the green except for the pulse and respiration rate which were edging towards the red.

'Wait a minute,' Charlie said suddenly. 'The sub has slowed. I'm not sure, but it seems to be moving back more into the shelter of the island's base.'

'That would make sense,' Jack interjected. 'If they can get close enough, they could take a chance on any sonar waves being scrambled enough by the bottom to hide them. How far away now?'

Charlie considered. 'I'd say close to five hundred yards. Wait ... I'm pretty sure they've stopped ... they seem to be about seventy feet higher, but not resting on the bottom.'

'Okay,' Keilty said tiredly, 'let's go before they decide this place is too unhealthy. It should take about five minutes.'

The three swam on again, pushing bodies that were close to exhaustion. Even for Charlie, the depth and the cold were beginning to make their effects felt. It was still impossible for the men to make out shapes, but Charlie kept up a running countdown for their benefit. When they were within fifty yards, he stopped them.

'It's just ahead,' he announced.

Keilty dragged his mind away from the torture of swimming and back to the sub.

'Can you see any indications of movement?'

'No, it's just sitting there. Those things at the back ... propellers ... aren't moving either. I can see it clearly, but nothing is happening.'

'Mort, you sound pretty beat ...'

'Shut up,' Keilty growled savagely. 'What the hell do you expect?'

Weston ignored the outburst and fumbled for his arm.

'What the devil are you doing?' Keilty tried to pull his arm away.

'Relax, you idiot. Take these . . .' He pressed two capsules sealed in plastic into Keilty's hand.

'What . . . ?'

'Don't argue. I've just taken two. They're a fancy pep pill. You too, Charlie, they won't hurt you.' He pressed two capules out of the plastic wrapper into the dolphin's mouth.

Keilty slipped up his mouthpiece and downed his. 'Okay, happy? Now, get out those limpet bombs. You guys know the drill, so let's go.'

Charlie started forward again. He would place each man at his station, and then take the stern himself. He was surprised at how much better he was beginning to feel. The cold had stopped bothering him, and all but a trace of sluggishness was gone. His sonar was now indicating a long object directly ahead and he backed carefully with his flukes to keep from swatting Keilty, then let their momentum carry him forward.

Keilty brushed the slick and cold surface of metal below him and felt around for a handhold. It must be *the* sub, he thought. If it had been sunk in the war, the hull would be crusted with marine growth. The blackness surrounding him was complete and utterly intense. The pains in his chest had stopped and he no longer felt as if he were freezing to death.

'Where are we?' he asked, keeping his voice down.

'Almost even with the forward hatch, about thirty feet from the bow.'

Keilty patted Charlie's flanks. 'Right on target, ol' buddy.'

Charlie moved ahead until he was directly over the hatch and paused. Jack unclipped the line and reached around to find the hatch. His fingers encountered the raised hinge and he pulled himself down.

'Here's where I get off. Good luck and see you later.'

Keilty felt the line go slack and Charlie again moved off.

As they made their way slowly aft towards the conning tower, Charlie broke the silence that had settled over them as Jack had dropped off.

'They won't have a chance, will they?'

Keilty hesitated. He could now feel the bulge of the conning tower against his hands and knew that precious seconds were wasting away.

'No,' he answered shortly. 'And besides, the answer to that is rather obvious. All those people on the receiving end of the bombs wouldn't have a chance either.'

'Another case of the greatest good for the greatest number?'

Keilty was taken aback by Charlie's reply. 'You know, kid, sometimes you surprise me.'

'And equally sometimes I surprise myself. Don't forget, swim straight up after you set the mines.'

Before Keilty unclipped his mike lead, the dolphin was gone. He fumbled at his belt and unclipped the first mine. He punctured the air sac with the point of his knife and turned the timer knob all the way to the right. He considered where to put it, then shrugged and pressed it against the conning tower wall near the base and activated the electromagnet. Hanging on with his finger tips, he felt his way down to the side of the sub, around the curve of the ballast tank, and stopped. He decided that right at the juncture would be a good spot, and set the timer. He placed the mine on the hull and flicked on the electromagnet.

A bright beam of dazzling light suddenly stabbed ahead through the darkness and he lost his grip, flailing wildly. He caught himself and shot down the side of the tank into the purient darkness. He waited a moment until his pulse rate started to slack off and then he inched back up, letting his eyes adjust to the unaccustomed brightness.

The light came from an underwater searchlight mounted high on the conning tower and drove a narrow, sharply defined cone straight ahead. He made his way slowly to deck level, where he was hidden in the shadows, and cautiously poked his head over. He caught the hollow rasp of a hatch being lifted and saw an oversized entryway about ten feet ahead of the conning tower being thrown back.

As he watched, a large metal canister poked over the coaming, rotated slowly, then rose until it was about ten feet above the deck. A second searchlight, mounted under the canister, also came to life and threw a powerful beam that reached out to bathe a portion of the deck and then swung quickly around to where he crouched. He ducked his head back just as the beam stabbed across the edge of the deck.

The darkness outside of the beam's narrow cone was barely relieved. He glanced at the luminous dial on his watch. Thirty-five seconds since he had set his first mine. Both Jack and Charlie should be well on their way to the surface by now. Keilty hesitated. Jack's mines should have less than a minute to go. He assumed that some type of TV system was enclosed in the canister, but why had it appeared? Had they heard him? And if so, what could they do about it? He could clearly make out the red casing of the bomb mounted on the conning tower. Even if they did see it, they could not do anything about disarming it.

His mind was working furiously as he reviewed the various possibilities. Even if they found the bomb he set, would they suspect that there were others? How fast could they fire those missiles? Even if they got one away. . . . He cursed the cruiser. They had probably been warned. . . . Even as he inched his head over the decking again, he heard a dull rasping sound. The metal canister turned to point back along the bow, the second searchlight following it until it shone full on an opening hatch.

A short – very short-lived – feeling of relief washed through him as he realized that they had not heard the mines being planted. They were only checking the hatch that covered the missiles. They had to make sure it was operating properly.

Keilty looked again at his watch. Fifty seconds before the first mine would go off. How long did it take to fire one of those deadly babies whose palely gleaming nose cones he could now see fully exposed? A cloud of gas bubbles burst out of the hatch and shot upwards. That answered his question. They were all set.

About forty seconds, his watch mocked him. And he'd better get the devil out of there or he'd blow up with the sub.

He had just started to push away, when a second sustained cloud of bubbles rose out of the hatch from around the missile nearest to him.

Within his body a combination of the high oxygen, deep pressure, and most important, the total frustration of his situation, snapped. He felt it like the kick of a glass of akvavit knocking him from sober to drunk. Berserk is a little-understood term in human psychology, but there exists such a mental state. Ask most Medal of Honor winners. The old Viking and Teutonic warriors cultivated and trained the trait. It is better than any of the so-called pep pills going, because it is instantaneous. With Keilty, as he saw the cloud of pressurized gas that would blow the first of the missiles clear, the total frustration of effort, more than any other item, was all that was needed. He forgot the pressure, the cold, his tired and aching body – all that was left was the will, somehow, to destroy that missile.

He snatched the limpet mine away from the juncture of hull and ballast tank, with the electromagnet full on. With a powerful push from his left hand, he vaulted over the edge of the decking and shot for the hatch.

The enemy crew must have seen him as he came in range of the camera, but there was nothing they could have done. He caught the edge of the hatch, disappearing in the cloud of bubbles, and somersaulted into the yawning hatch to slap the limpet mine against the casing of the missile.

Keilty paused only long enough to wedge his knife into the hatch coaming; then he was swimming furiously for the surface. Seconds later, the first and second mines went off, simultaneously with the launching of the missile.

The submarine, lifted by the bow with the first explosion, heeled sharply to the right with the second. But the first missile was away. Seconds later, the two midship mines exploded one after another and the submarine rippled along its length, tearing itself to pieces. Water pressure finished her off as surely as a nuclear bomb would have done. The fifth mine went off, more as an afterthought, and the sixth, if it did explode, did not register on Keilty's almost unconscious mind.

He was two hundred yards away when the shock waves from the explosives hit him. The sharp concussion from the amatol and the Deta-sheet explosive charges were magnified many times over in the crushing pressure.

Keilty, only semiconscious, was dimly aware that he was sinking. His arms and legs refused to respond to the feeble commands from his brain. A gray blankness suffused his vision, and somewhere in the deep recesses of his mind, he knew he had to force himself to swim, or die on the sea bottom now less than a hundred feet below. He tried again, and one arm pushed forward. A second force of will and a leg kicked feebly, but then the grayness closed in, bringing complete unconsciousness.

CHAPTER SIXTEEN

Jack Weston set the switch on the second mine and felt for the rear coaming of the torpedo tube. Satisfied, he twisted around until his body was pointing back along the length of the sub and began swimming, his left hand trailing along the steel hull. Finally, figuring that he had moved far enough back for the mine to explode into the forward torpedo storage room, he stopped and carefully pressed the mine against the hull and turned on the electromagnet.

He took a quick look over his right shoulder, but as he expected, he could see nothing beyond the reach of his light beam. He checked the mine placement once more with the underwater torch. Then, inflating a small air sac for added buoyancy, he kicked quickly upward towards the surface a thousand feet away. Hopefully, somewhere along the line, Charlie would meet him. Otherwise, it would be a long climb.

The three of them had been swimming vigorously below a thousand feet for over ten minutes. Between the pressure, numbing cold, and the first touch of shock signaling that his body had been ill-used too long, his mind was beginning to adopt the to-hell-with-it-what-do-I-care attitude that he knew could come from prolonged use of the 'lung' – essentially oxygen narcosis. The percentage of oxygen dissolved in his blood at these depths was too great for his body to handle. The 'lung' and its effects on human physiology were still much too new for anything definitive to be known, but he knew that unless he surfaced soon, he never would, and would never know it. With an effort requiring almost his total will, he kept swimming slowly upward.

Time to him became a hazy, useless tool. He was aware that he had long since stopped kicking, but he was borne up faster and faster by the inflated air sac. A long, rumbling roar reached him from the depths and he knew that the sub had been destroyed. An indeterminate time later, he realized that the darkness was beginning to lighten, until at fifty feet he was in a kind of twilight darkness in which a pale white light suffused everything. By now, his mind was void of everything except reaching the surface. Only the intense pain in his ears and chest penetrated to his conscious mind, warning him to stop, to release the air sac. With his knife, he cut the nylon cord, and relieved of his weight, it shot away from him.

Weston hung limply in the water, hands and feet paddling feebly to keep him from sinking slowly back. The pain of the mild decompression brought him somewhat to his senses. He peered closely at his watch, trying to make out the fuzzy numerals that wavered in the current.

He considered firing a transmitter, but was too exhausted to do more than fumble with the steel clip that held the pistol to his harness. Several more minutes passed and the pain lessened and he began trudging upward again. He wondered briefly about Charlie and Keilty, then forgot them as he made out the dim rippling ahead that meant the surface.

His head broke through and he tore away the mask and gulped air greedily. Then he trod water slowly for several minutes, retching feebly, until his stomach was completely empty. He cursed the burning taste of bile, and retched again.

'Tol' him I don't eat breakfast.'

His heart was beating furiously, thudding against his rib cage until the pain was almost unbearable. Slowly, he resolved the reason by forcing himself to concentrate. He rolled clumsily onto his back to get the 'lung' under water. The haze was thickening and his chest pained terribly as his overloaded heart strove to pump blood through the now useless 'lung'.

He could reach the hose connection, but the coupling defied his meager strength. Summoning his last particle of will power, he twisted it free and broke the connection, and fainted. Minutes later, he regained consciousness. His breathing was slowly returning to normal, but he was completely exhausted.

Again, driving his body, he forced himself to look around to see if he could get his bearings. The rain had started again, only this time as a fine misty spray that felt warm on his water-wrinkled face. The waves were still six to eight feet and occasionally he could catch a brief glimpse of Atuk Island, less than two miles away.

The island proper was hidden by the rain and low clouds, but the waves breaking over the reefs warned him of the dangers in trying to reach the safety of dry land by swimming, even if he had the strength.

He peered through the mist for several minutes, still treading water feebly. Charlie should be coming for him just about any time. He thought about putting the mask back on and ducking down for a look, but lacked the strength. He opened his fingers, or rather they opened of their own accord, and the mask slipped from his grasp. He watched stupidly as it sank from sight. Then he unsnapped the weight belt and let it sink after the mask. He considered briefly hanging onto the 'lung', then decided against it. The oxygen cylinder was empty and the gear would be just so much more dead weight. If he had long to wait, he could never stay afloat.

He shrugged out of the straps, unfastened the pack, and let the tanks drop away . . . then cursed himself for a fool. The mouthpiece held the underwater microphone as well as the ear-plug connection for Charlie's transphonemator and the jack for the transmitter cartridges.

He had just gone and done himself out of his only remaining means of communicating with the cruiser. Now he would have to wait until Keilty could surface and get a message off – providing Charlie could find them both.

Weston glanced at the watch on his wrist. He had been up nearly five minutes – fourteen minutes since the mines had gone off, and Charlie still had not shown up. Now he was really beginning to worry. He looked around at the choppy sea, which was empty in every direction, as far as he could see. Except for the slap of waves against his body, there was not a sound to be heard. The mist was fine enough to blend quietly with the waves. Its muffling quality was certain to shut out the sound of either the copter or the MTBs until they were almost on top of him.

He inflated both of the plastic air pillows he carried, hooked his arms through the straps, and centered them around his chest and back. Then, with a package of dye in one hand and the Very pistol with a magnesium flare in the chamber in the other hand, he settled back to wait and recoup his strength as best he could.

Charlie set the last of his two mines and backed away. He could see Weston swimming for the surface nearly fifty feet above the sub, as well as Keilty planting his last mine. He noted Jack's course and decided to move upwards where he could continue to keep an eye on both.

The cold had penetrated his wet suit and his throat and lungs were beginning to hurt quite badly. Charlie had never been this deep before and the cold and pressure squeezing him from all sides plus the visual blackness were steadily increasing his nervousness. His movements were becoming jerky and he could no longer think clearly without having to fight to keep his thoughts in mind.

He stopped moving upwards at seven hundred feet and hung suspended, tail slanting downward, as if he were a weary rocket pausing in its journey. In the seeming long swim up, depression and weariness had set in quickly as the pep pills wore off. He could no longer find Jack with his sonar and his apathy was so great that he felt it unimportant to search farther for him. It was easier to assume he was still moving upward and was now out of range.

He had no way of clearly estimating the time that had passed since the mines had been set, and as he set to work on the problem, the thought of Keilty flickered through his mind.

Languorously, he turned himself until his head was pointing downward. He was aware that he was sliding back as his tail flukes continued to move slowly up and down in the attitude he had used for station keeping, and he made himself stop. He exerted himself and pulsed his sonar tightly, circling slowly until he found the sub. He had to force himself to concentrate, or else he would have begun swimming slowly ahead again, only dimly aware that he was moving downward.

He could see the sub clearly now, outlined sharply against the faint background echo from the muddy bottom. It lay almost directly beneath him like a great metallic whale, completely silent, until he realized suddenly that a tiny figure just showed near the side. As his mind cleared slightly, he saw a hatch slide back, then the tiny figure dart forward into the opened hold. Then he found himself watching a figure approach from a great distance. A stream of froth bubbled around the forward deck of the submarine and rumbled back along the submarine's sides. As he watched, uncomprehending, a slender pencil darted at him, rushing past at less than two hundred yards as it slanted towards the surface. The submarine lurched and disappeared in a churning mass of released air.

Charlie smiled and felt good. Somewhere in his brain a relay clicked and he knew he had done a good job. For some reason which he could not understand, he knew his friend would be proud of him. He smiled foolishly again and turned to swim towards the surface. He felt out of breath and needed some air.

As he turned, he caught sight of the figure he had seen near the sub. It was twisting slowly from side to side as if helpless. A momentary surge of panic caught at him, but his instincts, nurtured and trained carefully, checked him. The shape was beginning to settle back, and for some reason it looked to him like another dolphin. The metal tanks were the same as he wore and the soft covering also resembled the one he wore. That dolphin was hurt and sinking and would drown.

He started down, his tail flukes working feebly at first, then more strongly as his instincts pushed him to make speed. He came abreast of the figure, but his sonar was jumbled as his mind wandered and his eyes could not see in the blackness that surrounded him. He fumbled with his beak at the unseen *man* until he found the center of gravity. Pausing shortly to set himself, he came beneath and started upward. His mind had stopped functioning and only his long past and insistent training told him that somehow this figure meant something, made him go on, climbing upward.

Brief tactile sensations brushed his unseeing mind: cold, blackness, the blankness that surrounded him as his sonar stopped functioning, and the deadly weariness. He climbed ever so slowly, his great reserves of strength draining away. By the time they broke surface nearly a half hour later, Charlie's head had cleared somewhat with the decrease in pressure. Keilty remained unconscious and Charlie struggled to keep his still form above the surface.

His powerful body floundered feebly, as if great weights were dragging him downward again. A fine rain pattered against his wrinkled face, hissing down softly, and every so often a wave washed over him completely. Otherwise there was only the gentle hissing and the soft lapping. He tried to look around, struggling to discern features in the watery scape surrounding him, but the red glow of the horizon pulsated and blended with the distant hammering in his brain. He realized in a sudden instant of clarity that he could no longer see. The reddish haze enveloped him and he felt the heavy burden slipping from his grasp.

Then it was gone. He thrashed wildly and his side brushed past something. Then a hand fumbled under his stomach. The red haze parted vaguely and the weight that had been dragging him downward fell away. He felt the mist again dimly as his back broke above the surface.

Then he realized he could breathe fresh air again and the dull ache in his back was gone. He lay on the surface and shuddered in convulsive spasms.

When he could see clearly again, Jack was stripping the 'lung' pack from Keilty's back and trying to fasten it to his air pillows at the same time. He swam to the two men and gripped the belt of Keilty's tunic in his teeth. Weston said something, but he missed it. Then Weston was back and inflated Keilty's air sacs and tied them beneath his chest. Charlie backed off and lay exhausted by even this brief exertion and watched Weston.

Jack unzipped Keilty's tunic and pressed his ear to his chest and listened for a long moment, then peeled back an eyelid. He looked helplessly at Charlie and was met only with a blank stare. He looked around wearily at the gentle sea and hidden sky, as if for help. Reaching a decision, he fumbled his kit up to where he could see it and pulled out an ampule of cortisone. He bit off the tip, not noticing the trickle of blood that started from his cut lips, and spat out the glass sliver, then slipped the needle on the end.

He pulled the tunic down enough to expose part of Keilty's upper shoulder and jabbed the needle into the vein and pushed the plunger home. He thought for a moment, then pulled a small chemical heat pad from the kit, broke the seal, and zipped it beneath the tunic, directly over Keilty's heart. There was nothing else he could do.

He glanced at Charlie, then reached out for the life line still trailing from Charlie's back and used it to tie the three of them together. Then he turned to Charlie.

'How are you feeling, ol' buddy?' he asked, his anxiety and exhaustion overshadowing the light tone of his voice.

Charlie stared dully back, unable to remember who or what this man meant to him. He knew it was a man, and that this was somehow significant, yet he could not tie the two concepts together. He closed his eyes, feeling the gentle rocking motion of the waves. He was dimly conscious of Jack's hands fastening two air pillows around him and momentarily he was grateful, at the same time hoping Keilty would be all right. Then the answer was lost to him and he slipped into unconsciousness.

Jack patted his sleek sides gently, then looked around for Keilty's 'lung' pack. He needed the microphone jack for the transmitter cartridges. But the tank had floated away and he caught a glimpse of it several feet off as it crested a slow wave.

He panicked for a moment and charged after it, but was brought up short by the combined weight of Charlie and Keilty. He went under and surfaced coughing. Then he began swimming slowly in the direction of the tank, towing the others after him. He did not dare free himself from the life line for fear he would lose them. He swam steadily on until he was able to grab a trailing strap.

The mist continued to drift down, smoothing the gently rolling waves that were beginning to show traces of a slowly rising oil slick. A piece of wooden panel bobbed to the surface several feet away, but Jack paid no attention to it. His nose had started to bleed and a reddish-brown tinge appeared beneath his left ear. His beaten body was too insensitive to feel the pain from his tortured chest and lungs as his heart thumped savagely. As he worked with the transmitter to assemble it, he was unaware of the deepening haze that was surrounding him. His leaden fingers fumbled with the microphone lead and he managed to croak a single sentence hoarsely into the recorder.

He fired the transmitter rocket, then followed it with a magnesium flare. He saw it burst into fantastic brilliance before a tiny blood clot found its way into the carotid artery and slipped upward into his brain.

CHAPTER SEVENTEEN

The bridge lookout on the *Vigilant* spotted the faintly burning magnesium halfway up the horizon through the thickening rain. Captain Whittlson ordered the co-ordinates transmitted to the two MTBs and the helicopter covering the area in a search pattern.

'It looks like at least one of the men is all right if they got a flare away,' Collins muttered. 'The dolphin certainly could not have fired the pistol.' He and Rawingson were staring through binoculars at the fading white glow against the watery sky.

Rawingson grunted. He could feel the deck shift beneath his feet and begin to come up as the ship's engineer responded to full emergency ahead. He was worried. Over forty minutes had passed since they had detected the explosion of the submarine, then moments later, the explosion that ripped apart the missile as it screamed for altitude.

That had followed the tensest, most stomach-tearing quarter hour that he had ever experienced. Keilty's terse recorded message that they were still moving in and for them to get the hell out, had brought the huge cruiser gliding to a standstill, its diesel engines shut down, its missiles tracking onto the hoped-for position of the sub and possible flight paths of the missiles.

Then the sonar operator had clamped his earphones tighter and kicked up the gain. The hydrophones were patched in and the ship's crew felt, rather than heard, the long, drawn-out bass rumble of the exploding submarine at one thousand feet.

Then the radar operator's agonized groan as the plot showed the missile break the surface and ignite. Before the first interceptor could be launched, it winked from the screen and one of the MTBs reported a brilliant flare ten miles from them as the missile exploded and fell harmlessly into the sea.

After that, more fear-filled silence as the cruiser and the MTBs converged on the helicopter's co-ordinates.

Rawingson took a deep breath and put down the glasses.

'How long, Captain . . . ?'

Whittlson lowered his glasses. 'About six minutes yet, Admiral. The first MTB should be there in less than four minutes.'

Rawingson turned back to the bank of windows. 'Yeah, if we can find them in this pea soup,' he muttered, half to himself.

'Radar should be able to help us this time, Admiral,' Whittlson remarked, his tone more hopeful than certain. 'The waves are rather low and there shouldn't be too much scatter,' he finished lamely.

'Sonar,' he growled, 'anything on that sonarbuoy yet?'

'No, sir, nothing. I don't think they released it.'

The three men continued to stare ahead, oblivious to the soft hum of conversation that flowed from the command consoles to every part of the cruiser, to the MTBs, and to Atkins in the helicopter.

The rain thickened until the mist became discrete particles of water that flowed down as softly as had the mist, yet it was more intensely obscuring. Visibility was now limited to several hundred feet and the spreading dye, timed to release from Charlie's packs after one hour, bubbled gently until it mingled with and was diluted by the floating patches of lubricating oil that dotted the surface.

One patch of oil and dye floated on the gentle current. This particular current originated far to the north between Japan and the Asiatic mainland and flowed sluggishly south until it mixed with the hundreds of other discrete streams that flowed into the mouth of the strait. As this single current passed around Atuk Island, it split in two distinct parts. The dolphin and the two humans were approaching this juncture, still more than two miles distant from the reefs surrounding the island. It created, in effect, a giant Venturi that caused the lighter oil and dye to move faster until, instead of pacing the three still forms, it lapped about them until they were directly in the center of the pool.

Charlie came to with a start, his mouth filled with an at-once-familiar cloying sensation. Instinctively, he shook his head to clear it, and the sudden movement brought him abruptly back to consciousness. He lay still for several seconds, trying to remember where he was. Then the oil on his lips began to sting fiercely, and he shook his head again and plunged beneath the surface to rinse the pain away.

The drag on his harness brought him up again quickly and he took a deep breath and saw the two bodies supported by the air cushions, their heads out of the water and mouths open in a grim parody of breathing.

He moved quickly to first Keilty, then Weston. Both seemed to be still alive, but he could not tell. He shook his head again and looked around, surprised at how sluggishly his body responded. Memory came flooding back and he knew where he was and why, but not how. The last thing he remembered was heading for the surface, a strong and biting pain clamping itself around his lungs.

Then he wondered where the hell the boats were. He ducked below the surface, but could not pick up the dull rumbling of the sonarbuoy. It hadn't been released. Did anyone know where the devil they were? He nosed at Keilty, then at Jack. Keilty's Very pistol was still clipped to his harness, but Weston's was missing.

He wondered how in hell *he* was going to fire a flare. Once again he ducked below the surface, but could not get deep enough to receive a decent sonar echo. He was barely three feet beneath, and the signal was lost in backscatter from the choppy surface. Charlie paused, then tried to swim deeper. He needed at least eight feet to minimize the backscattering echoes for any sizeable range, but the limp bodies supported by the air pillows brought him up short, and try as he might, he could get no deeper. Finally, just about out of breath, he surfaced again. The sluggishness was beginning to leave him, but he still felt torpid and his body refused to answer properly.

Charlie rested on the surface, considering the ridiculous predicament. First of all, the sonarbuoy was gone. Jack must have been verging on unconsciousness to have let the buoy sink without activating it. It had been attached to Jack's harness, and if his own condition was any example, then Jack must have been near complete exhaustion when he found the two of them. And he had probably been fully occupied in releasing them both from the dead weight of their gear. Charlie reached a dead end in his thinking. He knew that with the primitive human sonar equipment aboard the cruiser, that it would be close to a miracle if they were found. The rain was getting thicker and the seas were beginning to chop more strongly than when they had submerged.

The problem then, was to somehow get the two men and himself to safety. He did not know their condition for certain, but neither had moved and he assumed it was extremely bad. He also knew that they could not be expected to spend more than one or two hours longer in the open ocean without dying. In spite of the wet suit, *he* was beginning to chill rapidly – and he had a good thick layer of insulation.

Charlie set about reviewing this new set of data, evolved from the present situation. There were several islands in reach. He thought he would be able to tow the two men to the nearest and find a way through the reef. But then what? Keilty had not told him whether they were inhabited. If they were not, what would he do with Keilty and Weston? Charlie was sure they needed medical attention and he would not be able even to get them onto dry land. The hope would be that one of them would regain consciousness and fire a flare. But on the other hand, wasn't there an equal chance that they would be found where they were? Charlie realized that the more he thought, the more confused he became. He wondered finally what it would be like to have hands.

He nosed first at Keilty, then at Jack. No response. Then he swore for a while until he felt better. Then he tried to figure out a way to use the pistol, with only his teeth to work with.

The rain was now definitely coming down harder. The drops were kicking up small ripples as they slanted down into the choppy waves. The wind had dropped away to nothing and again the only sound was that of the rain. Charlie noticed with a start that it was getting darker, then remembered that it would be getting along close to evening. He made a decision.

At least they stood some kind of chance with the island. Charlie turned slowly, pulling the two men into line until Keilty humped along, slightly behind Weston. At least the air pillows kept their heads out of the water. He began swimming slowly forward, surprised at the drag the two limp bodies created.

It was completely dark. Charlie lay exhausted, unable to swim another stroke. He retched feebly and then his body broke into a series of shuddering convulsions, all the more terrible because they wasted the last bit of energy stored in the sleek, gray body. Finally he lay quietly on the surface, riding with the rise and fall of the waves. The rain had increased until it was falling now with a steady drumming. With the return of the always vagrant wind, now stiffening to a mild gale, the waves had picked up until they were short swells four to six feet high that broke occasionally, washing over the three still figures.

Once again, Charlie nosed at the two men, and again, no response. Charlie guessed they were rapidly reaching the end. While it was still light enough to see, he had noticed a pale bluish tint to Keilty's lips and skin. Now another hour had passed and still nothing. And as far as he could tell, towing the heavy bodies, he had made almost no headway towards the island. After an hour and a half of swimming, he still could not hear the surf which should have roared as it broke on the reefs surrounding the island. The current was carrying them along on its southeastern leg, and by swimming with it, Charlie had gained nearly three miles, but only half a mile toward the island itself.

Now he had only enough strength to turn Keilty and Weston so that they were sheltered in the lee of his body. He was nearing unconsciousness himself, he knew, from exhaustion, and what was worse, from shock. He felt himself slipping into sleep. He wondered idly again, as he had many times in the past two hours, if he could get deep enough to find the ships with sonar. But even if he found them, the knowledge wouldn't help him, because he had no way of signaling their position. Sleep closed in as he drifted further and further into black nothingness, except for a clamoring somewhere in his mind. What was it? . . . he fought back up . . . something that he had thought . . . something . . . then he had it. *Sonar*. His sonar. He did not need it to find the ships. They needed it to find him.

Sleep brushed at him again and his eyes closed slowly. Then he was awake again. He couldn't sleep. They would all die here, unless . . . He moved awkwardly and submerged, his lower jaw drawn in as tightly as possible, and he began his echo – ranging at a wide angle. The echoes roared back from the surface in a cacophony of signal noise that roared and screamed pain in his skull. He did not need to locate anything, just create a sonar disturbance in as localized an area and at as low a frequency as possible. His lowest band length was near the upper limits of human sonar gear. The pain screamed at him, competed with the sleep of exhaustion for possession of his mind, but he knew if he stopped, he would sleep and they would all die.

They had to be listening. Fifteen minutes later, the great dolphin passed out.

CHAPTER EIGHTEEN

Rawingson sank onto the padded swivel stool, his eyes red-rimmed and heavily circled from peering through the binoculars. He stared dully at the consoles backed along the aft bulkhead of the bridge. The sweat-stained shirts of the console operators clung to their backs as they slumped wearily, yet alert, peering at their instruments. The radar monitor had channeled his sweep image to a large display screen over the bridge's forward ports, while he continued to stare at the smaller console screen, his fingers playing delicately over the keyboard as he directed the beam along its vectored search pattern. Nothing showed on the twin image that flickered above their heads but the small dots marking the location of the MTBs, making a visual search, and at the end of every sweep, the diffused bulk of Atuk Island to the north.

The elapsed-time chronometer showed three hours and sixteen minutes since the search had begun.

The met. report, stuck to the magnetized bulletin board, mocked him. The water temperature was down to 67° F., eight degrees below the normal temperature for these equatorial waters. The air temperature was 66° and the wind at twenty-three knots. The cold front had swept southerly in a matter of hours from off the Indonesian island chain, pushing the monsoon south again, but worsening survival conditions for the men and the dolphin. *If* there was any hope remaining at all.

The rain was steady as the cruiser plowed steadily towards Atuk Island at five knots. Shortly they would swing around to move west in an ever-narrowing square search pattern.

Rawingson tried again to guess at the innumerable conditions that could keep the men silent, yet still alive. His best guess was that, no matter what, their time was running out. They would be exhausted, and at 67° F. they would not last long unless fully conscious. And if they were conscious, why hadn't they signaled again?

His thoughts were interrupted as the radioman handed a flimsy to Whittlson. He paraphrased it slowly:

'The *Saratoga* is moving down from the South China Sea. They are going to launch two specially equipped aircraft for night search, which should reach us in little less than two hours.'

He looked helplessly at Rawingson. Before Rawingson could answer, the sonar operator grabbed his headphones, then flicked a switch that filled the bridge with a curious rumbling roar over its PA system.

'What the hell?' Collins growled, swinging around quickly to stare at Rawingson.

The sonar operator turned and half lifted an earphone. 'We're picking up a strange sonar signal, sir. It's full of echoes and subechoes and right near the top end of the bandspread.'

He turned back to the console, fingers playing swiftly over the keys; the sound fluctuated once, then died away abruptly.

'Did you get a fix?' Rawingson rapped out.

'Aye, sir, bearing two-nine-six at fourteen miles, three hundred feet and some odd . . . just a moment, sir . . . three hundred and twenty feet.'

Rawingson could see the electronic star marker on the overhead screen settle on the spot designated, close to the blip marking the island.

Rawingson was puzzled momentarily; then he shot out of his seat and was across the bridge. 'Captain!' Rawingson roared as he moved to the radar console. 'That might be them using the dolphin as a sonar marker.'

The radar operator carefully narrowed his sweep to the designated area, cranking the successively narrowing image up in magnification to fill the screen. Then Rawingson saw them: three fluctuating blips, very faint, almost invisible.

'That might be them, sir. The flickering could be caused by the waves.'

Rawingson let out his breath in one long hiss. Collins and Whittlson flanked him on either side, bending over the radar operator to watch the three, sometimes two, or one, blips flickering on the glowing screen.

'Helm, round on a course of two-nine-six, flank emergency,' Whittlson rapped out. 'Wireless, pass the information and exact location to the MTBs, and have four-oh-three get to them immediately. What is his exact range?'

'Little over four miles, sir . . .'

Rawingson found that his knees were refusing to support him and stumbled back to the chair. For the third time that day he felt the cruiser plummet ahead at close to forty-five knots. A shudder passed through his body and a moment of utter detachment cut him loose from the bridge; then he was sitting in the chair, trying to calm his hands that insisted on shaking so badly he could not light a cigarette.

MTB 403 idled alongside the three still forms. Two life-jacketed sailors went over the side and swam the few short feet separating them. In the dead illumination of the MTB's searchlight, the three bodies appeared to be awash in quietly rolling surf with occasional waves breaking to roll them to and fro. The two sailors reached the unconscious dolphin first and found the life line that tied them all together. Then the MTB was alongside and willing hands hauled them up one by one. As soon as they were stretched on the deck, the MTB came about in a tight turn and roared off to meet the approaching cruiser.

Four minutes later, the MTB was alongside and stretcher slings slammed down onto the deck. No time was wasted in preliminary examination. Keilty and Weston were quickly slipped into the stretchers and were away, while Charlie's tank, retrieved earlier from the helicopter, was dropped down onto the deck.

Rawingson rode with the ship's doctor as the tractor broke speed records in getting them into the sick bay.

CHAPTER NINETEEN

The parting tatters of rain drummed briefly on the eaves of the bungalow and died slowly away. Keilty, standing motionless at the window, watched quietly, his expression stonily fixed, as the gray rain receded to reveal first the spread of dull green lawn and then the beach. Beyond the beach, the open Gulf showed the last traces of mist being swept down into its colorless maw. Margaritta slept quietly on the couch behind him, feet drawn up and tucked against the back, the white blanket with which he had covered her contrasting dimly in the dull light with her hair.

Keilty continued to stand at the window, waiting for the sun to disperse the afternoon rain clouds. He watched a gull wheeling against the sky, his eyes tracking its flight as it shuttled between the waves and the clouds, but his mind did not register the image.

Quietly, he opened the sliding glass door and stepped out onto the patio. With the end of the rain, the light had improved. The white cover on his sloop attracted his eye and he started across the lawn towards the pier. The cool grass, covered with fine rain drops, felt good to his bare feet and he walked slowly until he reached the wooden deck. He unlashed the canvas cover and pulled it carefully onto the deck so as not to dump the water that had settled in its folds into the boat. After hanging it over the railing to dry, he stepped aboard, and skirting the cabin, went forward to loosen the bowline and check the forestays.

The jib was folded away in the sail locker and he fetched it out, cleated it to the forestay and slowly pulled it up to the mast. The stern line followed and he pushed the tiller over until the jib caught the first vestiges of the returning sea breeze and began to fill. The boat made headway, the rudder bit, and she began to move slowly towards the entrance in the coral reef.

Keilty brought the sloop up into the wind and she began to pick up speed as the breeze freshened. The boat cleared the low coral shelves at the entrance and quickened to the stronger breezes and dancing waves. Keilty lashed the tiller and raised the mainsail with strong, steady pulls. The sail cracked sharply, filled, and the sloop heeled and dug in.

With the tiller bar under his arm again, he stretched out, catlike, on the thwart and scrabbled in the locker for a cigarette. The sloop slipped on under the leaden sky as the island receded behind. From time to time, Keilty cupped the cigarette in his hand to protect it from the spray and watched the billowing shape of the mainsail. Finally, he felt a sharp pain from the cigarette ash and flicked the butt over the side.

The rain squall had freshened the air as it passed on, taking the humid heat of the still afternoon with it. The flashes of spray that were flung at him from the bow were curiously refreshing. Quietly, he sat quite still and thought for a long time.

He thought about Charlie – from the time they had first become associated until the dive to the submarine a week ago. He thought about their relationship. Curiously enough, there had never been any other relationship than that of friendship. But now, it had gone far beyond even that, not in a personal sense, but in a more encompassing arrangement. They had both become spokesmen for each other's kind and neither of them liked it. But Charlie had been forced into the position because of his relatively intimate contact with human beings. Keilty, because of Charlie.

Charlie had seen too much, discovered too much about the human race. He could clearly see that man would soon begin to displace him as intelligent life in the sea. The process might take thousands of years, but it would be inevitable. Already, there were three inhabited bases on the continental shelves: one off the United States, the San Clemente Base, and one off the Soviet Union in the Sea of Okhotsk, and a third undersea base, the French station under the Mediterranean. Sealab VI was already in progress at 12,000 feet in the Atlantic. And Charlie could read the handwriting on the wall. Just two days ago he had cataloged his reasoning by pointing out to Keilty that there was more oil, more fresh water and food, and more mineral deposits on the world's continental shelves than had been discovered so far on the continents themselves. He remembered Charlie's question . . . 'What do we do when man goes after this wealth? Will careful reasoning appeal to him while his civilization dies of thirst, hunger, and lack of power?'

He had had no answer then and had none now. Keilty did not know what Charlie could do about it, but he knew that man must not face this type of intelligence as an enemy, in the enemy's domain.

The wind had freshened perceptibly as the breeze, flowing in to fill the low-pressure area left by the departing storm, quickened. The wind had veered two points to the northeast, and Keilty pushed the tiller over and let the sails trim up. He now had a following wind blowing from the port quarter and the sloop dived into the seas like an angry shark. He concentrated his attention on handling the lively boat. The waves were running only two to three feet at crest, but with the wind behind, the sloop pitched strongly as the wind drew on the luff of the main and jib, and the yaw was almost nonexistent in the steady seas. He trimmed the jib a little tighter and felt the answering thrust as the sloop leaped ahead. Satisfied, he studied the curve of the jib, calculating the flow of the true wind through the Venturi-like gap between the jib and the main. Satisfied that the tremendous air pressure on the sails was correctly balancing the side thrust on the keel and that he was losing little motion to leeward, he settled back to enjoy the challenge to the elements that every sailor in human history has felt.

Out of the corner of his eye, he caught the shape of a dolphin coming up to breathe; then it was gone. Thoughtfully he watched for a second appearance, but none came.

'So it's begun,' he said half aloud to himself, and felt a sudden chill reach through him. He was being watched, as was every ship or boat in the area. In three short days, patrols, usually two dolphins to an area, were watching every movement of everything that floated in the Keys.

Keilty glanced up at the blue sky, burned almost coppery by the swift return of the sun. Above him hung only slow-moving remnants of clouds left by the squall, but low on the western horizon to starboard, the black line of squall clouds marched implacably on into the Gulf of Mexico. The appearance of the single dolphin had ruined the peace of mind the sloop had induced and he angrily gauged the waves and wind and threw the boat over on a starboard tack. With a clatter, the boom swung round over his head and the jib cracked sharply as it filled again. A long beat north by east, close-hauled, would put him a mile east and north of the island and he could come about again and drop down into the entrance. Bitterly he leaned back to wait out the long hour.

Forty-five minutes later, he could make out the surf breaking on the coral reef and the deep green, almost black of the island vegetation. Reaching off to the north was a long tongue of land, and when he came abreast of the tip, he brought the sloop around until it was moving along the reef half a mile out, towards the entrance.

He tried again, as he had many times in the last week since regaining consciousness in the *Vigilant*'s sick bay, to remember what had happened after the submarine had blown up. He remembered everything quite clearly up to the time he had set his last charge, but after that, it was all a blank.

He remembered the intense cold and the pain in his chest, and he thought he could remember snatches of incidents, particularly the concussion of the exploding charges. He was also quite certain that he remembered being pulled slowly through the water and feeling the rain beating down on his face. He was sure of this because he remembered being angry that he could not turn his head away.

But beyond that, he remembered only regaining consciousness in a darkened sick bay on the cruiser and the panic of disorientation before the doctor got to him. Then followed the two-day trip back to Singapore with the ship lurching in the heavy seas of the monsoon that had finally struck. He had watched, from a stretcher on the bridge, as Jack's flag-draped burial bag slid into the waves, and then had managed to walk the distance back to sick bay to report to the strangely disorientated dolphin.

Charlie had lain quietly in his tank all during the return voyage. And only the long flight across the Pacific had roused him to any semblance of his former character. Keilty would have sworn that he was tremendously preoccupied; and he was right. He himself wheeled Charlie's tank to the pen and helped him into the water. Charlie swam slowly up and down the pool for a few minutes before heading out to the reef. That was the last Keilty had seen of him.

The tide was running with him and the sloop cleared the narrow entrance to the reef and sailed into the lagoon. As he came around the shoulder of the island, Keilty could see a helicopter hovering for a landing. Keilty brought the sloop around for an approach and dropped the mainsail. As the sloop neared the deck, he let go the jib and coasted slowly in. A shore patrolman reached over with the boat hook and pulled the boat in and snubbed the bowline tight.

Rawingson waited quietly as he climbed over the rail and onto the dock. The two men walked slowly back to the terrace and into the bungalow. Keilty crossed the room and sank down on the couch, while Rawingson moved around the bar to fix two stiff drinks. He came back and handed one to Keilty and remained standing. Finally he asked, 'Are you feeling all right?'

Keilty lay back with his hands beneath his head and for long moments stared at the ceiling, ignoring the question; then he said quietly, 'Jack died because of this nonsense. And Charlie disappeared. God knows where he's gone or why . . .' His voice trailed off.

'Then I take it you still have no word from him?' One look at Keilty's expression and Rawingson said hurriedly, 'No, ignore that. It was a stupid question.'

Both men were thinking back over the events of the last three weeks, of the deadly brink of war that had been approached so closely. Rawingson did not know if it could have been averted without the dolphin's help or not, and he did not care. All that mattered was that the bombs had been destroyed before the millions of lives that were so vulnerable had been wiped out. He was thinking too, of the long discussions of the last week at the Pentagon, of the President's orders to develop a unit in the Navy that would use dolphins in much the same way as the K–9 corps uses dogs. He recalled too his fruitless arguments that dolphins could not, would not allow themselves to be used in this way. He had seen the strained, but polite smiles as he tried to explain the degree of intelligence inherent in the dolphin; the intense curiosity that Charlie displayed, coupled with his reluctance to enter into human affairs. His arguments that Charlie had done what he had done because of his friendship and regard for Keilty – for no other reason. He had tried time and time again to explain that Charlie knew little about human politics and cared less, that this démarche between the Western alliance and Communism was completely not understandable to him. All his arguments had fallen on deaf ears. To them, the issue was black and white.

He had left Washington with a promotion, orders, and a burning desire to return to the Keys for a rest. Keilty had replied to his cable immediately, and now he stood in the bungalow's living room, the sound of Margaritta's singing coming faintly to the house, and Keilty's haunted face before him.

He carefully searched that face, noting the pale gauntness, the staring eyes, red-rimmed from lack of sleep. The skin on his massive chest, while freshly sun-burned, betrayed the ordeal of the dive and the submarine's destruction, Charlie's disappearance, and Jack's death in the way it was shrunken tight over the startling rib cage. The immense bruise that still covered half his back and sloped over one shoulder indicated the fierce reaction of his body to the diving 'lung'. And he recalled the first day after the recovery of the two men and the dolphin, when the ship's surgeon had fought to save their lives. He had succeeded with the dolphin and Keilty, but Jack had suffered a stroke and his body defenses were too drained by the long ordeal. He had died without even recovering consciousness.

To break his mind away from that useless line of thought, he asked to hear the tape.

Keilty got up and went over to his desk and switched on the tape recorder. There was a moment of silence; then Charlie's voice, stiff and somehow formal, even coming through the transphonemator, filled the room. Rawingson listened quietly, pity flooding through him for Keilty as the dolphin's quiet voice talked on.

'My friend Mort. I am sorry that I must return at night to make this tape. I would like to see you again. I have a good bit of serious thinking to do about the events of the past few weeks. I feel that I am now strong enough to and in fact need to rejoin my family-herd in the open sea. Unfortunately, I cannot take you with me, nor would I if it were possible. I have much to think about and many questions to resolve.

'My old teacher, the herd guardian, will listen to me and possibly suggest a course of action. As has become clear to me, a decision must be made as to whether or not a close co-operation between our peoples is desirable. If it is not, I do not know what can be done, but something must and shall. Your own history indicates the inadvisability of attempting to keep two groups apart to avoid conflict. I hope this will never be, as strongly as I hope that we never become enemies, your race and mine. Remember, you once suggested that we were either a very advanced, or a very degenerate race. This is one of the questions I must resolve.

'I have felt something curious in knowing that Jack is dead and that I will never argue or swim with him again . . . is this what you mean by sorrow? Is this an emotion, what I feel now?

'I will come back . . . when, I am not sure. Until then, I leave you this tape recording.'

Rawingson and Keilty both continued to stare at the empty reel, long after the tape had run out.